Brett came to a halt, trying to figure out what was going on

Renita wasn't the type to flirt or flaunt her body, yet that's exactly what she was doing.

Thanks to his ex-wife, he was all too familiar with the body language of a woman on the prowl. Renita was preening, touching her hair, pushing her arms together and leaning on the table to emphasize her cleavage.

She was also drunk. When she raised her glass she nearly missed her mouth then giggled when a few drops of sparkling wine fizzed down her chin. No wonder she was acting this way. She didn't know what she was doing.

Her admirer immediately topped up her glass from a bottle on the table. Clearly he expected the evening to end with Renita in his bed.

Brett carefully set his beer on a nearby table.

Not bloody likely, mate.

Dear Reader,

Are you a couch potato or a fitness freak? Or are you somewhere in between? I fall into the "in between" category. I go to the gym regularly and walk almost every day. Even so, I struggle to keep my weight under control. Part of the reason is that I love to cook and, naturally, to eat. I enjoy little indulgences like a piece of chocolate or a glass of wine.

To me, achieving a healthy, happy lifestyle comes down to finding a balance, where feeling fit gives as much pleasure as having a nice meal. Health versus appearance; appearance versus personality; these are some of the other issues I've explored in the second book of the Summerside Stories trilogy, *In His Good Hands*.

Renita Thatcher is a couch potato trying to change her ways with the help of gym owner Brett O'Connor, who also happens to be her unrequited high school crush.

I hope you enjoy reading Renita's story and can identify with her journey from the couch to the gym.

I love to hear from readers. You can find me at www.joankilby.com or write to me c/o Harlequin Enterprises Limited, 225 Duncan Mill Road, Don Mills, ON, Canada M3B 3K9.

Joan Kilby

In His Good Hands
Joan Kilby

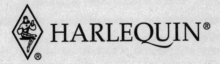

HARLEQUIN®

TORONTO • NEW YORK • LONDON
AMSTERDAM • PARIS • SYDNEY • HAMBURG
STOCKHOLM • ATHENS • TOKYO • MILAN • MADRID
PRAGUE • WARSAW • BUDAPEST • AUCKLAND

Recycling programs
for this product may
not exist in your area.

ISBN-13: 978-0-373-71687-6

IN HIS GOOD HANDS

Copyright © 2011 by Joan Kilby

www.eHarlequin.com

Printed in U.S.A.

ABOUT THE AUTHOR

Joan Kilby goes to her local gym several times a week for Body Balance—a combination of Tai Chi, pilates and yoga. And yes, there is a cappuccino machine where she and her friends hang out after class. Melbournians love their coffee! Like the hero in this book, Joan is mathematically challenged. Unlike the hero, she knows better than to mess around with large sums of money. Joan's husband and three children help keep her sane while she's writing. And her dog, Toby, takes her for a walk every day.

Books by Joan Kilby

HARLEQUIN SUPERROMANCE

 777—A FATHER'S PLACE
 832—TEMPORARY WIFE
 873—SPENCER'S CHILD
 941—THE CATTLEMAN'S BRIDE
 965—THE SECOND PROMISE
1030—CHILD OF HIS HEART
1076—CHILD OF HER DREAMS
1114—CHILD OF THEIR VOWS
1212—HOMECOMING WIFE
1224—FAMILY MATTERS
1236—A MOM FOR CHRISTMAS
1324—PARTY OF THREE
1364—BEACH BABY
1437—NANNY MAKES THREE
1466—HOW TO TRAP A PARENT
1681—HER GREAT EXPECTATIONS*

*Summerside Stories

To my gym/coffee buddies
Madeline, Deb, Anne, Carolyn and Sandy.
Thanks for the laughs and the friendship.
Saturday wouldn't be the same without you.

CHAPTER ONE

RENITA THATCHER TUGGED AT the jacket of her blue silk-blend suit, struggling to fasten it across her stomach. Cripes, if she got any bigger she'd have to wear a tent to work. Usually she left the jacket open, but a button had popped off her blouse.

Of all days—

Her office door burst open. Poppy, her young assistant, announced breathlessly, "Brett O'Connor's here."

"Already?" Renita sucked in her gut, tightened what stomach muscles she possessed, and squeezed the button through the hole. "Give me two minutes, then show him in."

Poppy left, closing the door behind her. Renita whipped a compact out of her top drawer and checked her hair, tucking a wavy dark strand behind her ear. She tried taking her glasses off. Nope, she was blind without them. Baring her teeth in the tiny mirror, she made sure there were no lipstick smears or sesame seeds from her breakfast bagel.

She put away her compact and took several deep breaths to slow her tripping heart, coaching herself not to get anxious over this meeting. Her high school crush on Brett O'Connor was ancient history. Anyway, he'd never been interested in her *that* way, so his visit was nothing to get excited about.

Sure, she was curious about why he'd returned to Summerside, but her biggest concern right now was that a) her jacket button didn't pop and b) she didn't reveal by a single word, gesture or look that she'd ever had the slightest hint of romantic feelings toward him.

Professionalism, that was the key. She was no longer a nerdy, chubby fifteen-year-old infatuated with the school jock who'd broken her heart. She was a businesswoman and the loans manager at Community Bank, just doing her job.

Poppy knocked. Renita's mouth felt as dry as the paper she was clutching in her damp palms as a prop. Poppy opened the door, ushering in Brett O'Connor, who was gorgeous as ever in a casual suit jacket over an open-necked shirt and designer jeans. He carried a manila envelope.

At the last second Renita remembered the jar of jelly beans and whisked it off her desk and into a drawer.

"Hello, Brett." She rose, grateful that her voice, at least, was cool and calm. The sight of his thick, sun-streaked hair and slightly crooked nose transported her straight back to grade eleven, when a passing glance from him in the school corridor had been enough to send her into dreamy reveries.

Not now, though. No way.

She extended a hand. "How are you?"

"G'day, Renita. It's been a while." His clasp was firm, almost painful, as if he didn't know his own strength, and his blue gaze so direct it was like a stab to the heart. "What is it, thirteen years?"

"Something like that." She gestured to a chair. "Tell me, what can I do for you?"

He sat, but instead of getting down to business, he leaned back and shook his head. "I can't get over it. You're exactly the same."

"Gee, thanks. And here I thought I'd improved."

He flashed her his easy grin. "You always had a wisecrack for every occasion."

"No, I only speak the truth," she deadpanned. "Everyone just thinks I'm joking."

"What I meant was you look fabulous." When she raised her eyebrows skeptically, he insisted, "Honestly, you do."

"Don't flatter me, Brett." Renita knew she was well-groomed, pretty but not beautiful. Most of the time she thought she looked just fine—well, except for the extra weight. But she didn't believe for one second that Brett, who was used to being mobbed by half-naked football groupies, could possibly think she looked *fabulous.*

"You look...*real,*" he amended, having the grace to appear sheepish at being called on his sincerity.

"Real. Yep, that's me." Real meant eyeglasses,

hair with a mind of its own, jackets that strained at the buttons.

She searched beneath his gorgeousness for signs that he'd aged badly from the debauched life he must have led as a professional football player. Not to mention Australian rules football was a rough sport. Brett had been hot in high school. Hotter still during televised football games, with his cheek smeared with dirt and his muscles—all sweaty and glistening—exposed by his sleeveless jersey and tight shorts. But apart from a small white scar across his right eyebrow, laughter lines around his eyes and mouth and the way his lanky frame had filled out with solid muscle, he looked pretty much the same as he had at seventeen. Sexy and athletic.

"So, Brett, are you here for a loan?"

"First I'd like to know how my favorite math tutor is doing," he said, still with that easy smile, that confidence that used to enthrall her. Now it only grated on her nerves.

He was trying to charm her. It came to him as easily as breathing, and probably just as unconsciously. It took her back to afternoons around her parents' farmhouse kitchen table. She had tried earnestly to teach him trigonometry; he had tried to distract her with jokes. She'd wanted to slap him.

Or kiss him.

"How could I be your favorite tutor?" She laughed nervously, although she was anything but amused.

"I dropped you two weeks before the final exam, remember?"

"Oh, yeah." Brett frowned. "Why did you do that, anyway?"

"Dad needed my help with chores after school," she lied, even as hurt and anger pushed their way to the surface.

What an idiot she'd been back then, imagining that just because they'd laughed together, just because he'd tweaked her ponytail, he'd *liked* her. She could still see his stunned expression, hear his excruciatingly blunt, "Sorry, you're not my type," when she'd asked him to the grade eleven dance.

"Is it a home loan or business loan you're after?"

"Your father used to put the fear of God into me whenever I came around," Brett went on, seemingly oblivious to her efforts to change the subject. "But I'll never forget the cakes and cookies your mum baked for our study sessions. How are your folks doing?"

"They sold the farm and moved into Summerside to be near Jack, Lexie and me," Renita said, summing up the past six months in a few quick words. What she didn't say was that her parents, Steve and Hetty Thatcher, weren't fine at all. They were having marriage problems, and her dad was sick. But she was done chatting. She shuffled some papers on her desk. "Interest rates are set to go up next month, so I'm recommending to our borrowers that they lock in for a fixed term."

"I ran into Jack yesterday in the grocery store,"

Brett added. "He told me your father had been in the hospital."

Renita nodded, biting her lip. The scare was recent enough that she was still shaken up over it.

"Is Steve all right?" Brett pressed. "Jack was in a hurry and didn't have time to tell me what happened."

She gripped her pen tightly between her fingers. "My dad's been diagnosed with type 2 diabetes."

Brett leaned forward, his clear blue eyes troubled. "I didn't think that usually meant a hospital stay."

Couldn't he just drop it? Renita met his gaze, and that was her undoing. His expression was so sympathetic she couldn't resist confiding in him. "Mum was away on a meditation retreat and Dad let his diet go to hell. No one knew he had diabetes or that he was eating a ton of sweets. Next thing, he was severely dehydrated and his blood sugar levels were through the roof. He was in a coma for two days."

"I'm sorry," Brett murmured. "Is he okay now?"

Sorry. Was he? Renita tapped the pen against her blotter. For reasons she'd never understood, Brett and her father didn't get along.

"He's out of the hospital. Mum's back home and taking care of him." Grudgingly. Hetty, and even Jack and Sienna, believed Steve had brought his illness on himself to punish her for going away.

"My gym is sponsoring the Diabetes Fun Run next month," Brett said. "You and Steve should think about entering."

"Me, run?" Renita laughed. "I'm built for comfort, not speed." She was like her dad in many ways, including having a weakness for sweets.

"It's not a race," Brett said. "It's to support a good cause. And an excuse to get some exercise."

Renita shifted uncomfortably, feeling her waistband pinch. Steve's health crisis had given her a jolt. She needed to do something about her weight or *she* might end up with type 2 diabetes. In fact, she was going on a diet. Starting next Monday. Or Tuesday.

Just thinking about being hungry made her cranky.

"I support the cause, but as for exercise, I'd sooner stick flaming bamboo shoots beneath my fingernails."

"Okay, I get the picture. I'm not here to torture you." Brett let the subject go. "What are you doing these days? Do you still see anyone from high school?"

"Most everyone has moved away." Didn't he get that they weren't friends?

"I'm looking forward to catching up with Jack and his fiancée," he said. "What's her name?"

"Sienna. Look, could we get down to business?" Renita sat up straighter to ease the strain on her jacket. "I'm sure your time is valuable, and I have another appointment coming up. Are you here about a bank loan?"

Silence followed her brusque request.

"I want to buy the Summerside Fitness Center,"

Brett finally admitted. "I've taken over managing the place and the owner's keen to sell."

"You must have just started there. I haven't seen you around town." Hadn't heard any buzz that Brett's minor celebrity status would have generated, either.

"That's right. We moved in last week, to a house on Cliff Road."

"We?" The word popped out before Renita could stop herself. Brett's divorce six months ago had been splashed all over the tabloids, but she wouldn't be surprised if he'd already found another girlfriend. "Sorry, your personal life is none of my business."

"You can ask. We're old friends." Another moment of silence passed, as if he expected her to agree. When she didn't, his blue eyes hardened. "My daughter, Tegan, and I."

"Oh, I see."

"Tegan wishes there were more fashion boutiques in Summerside, but I'm glad she can't spend all her time shopping." Brett rolled on, regaining his good humor. "With us practically living on the beach, she'll be able to learn to sail. Summerside is a good place to grow up, on the fringe between city and country. Well, you would know. You had a great childhood on the farm."

There he was, inviting Renita to reminisce again. She wasn't going to bite. "About the gym…I drive past there regularly. The building looks run-down. I hope it's going for a good price."

"Seven hundred and fifty thousand dollars. That

includes all equipment, such as it is. It's reasonable," Brett said. "But I'll need to completely refurbish the place. Exercise machines, flooring, coffee area, child care, change rooms—the works."

Finally, they were getting down to business. "Coffee?" Renita asked. "Isn't that encouraging unhealthy habits?"

"I gather this used to be a squash club. There's a small kitchen where players used to wait for a court." He shrugged. "I'm into fitness, but I'm not a fanatic. If people want coffee, they can have it."

"Is the gym currently running at a profit?"

"A very slim one. The place has been neglected since the owner moved to Sydney last year. His manager quit months ago and hasn't been replaced. One of the instructors has been in charge, but obviously, she can't do that justice and teach classes at the same time. Once I take over things will improve." Brett removed a sheaf of papers from his manila envelope and handed them to Renita. "I've worked up a statement of operating costs, revenue and expenses."

She scanned the detailed spreadsheets. "You've certainly done your homework."

"And this time without your assistance."

She glanced up. He was watching her with that half smile that used to turn her knees to jelly. The pages rattled faintly in her hands. "Let's hope you're better at math than you used to be."

Renita ducked her head and studied the figures.

She still found Brett physically attractive; a woman would have to be blind not to. But she was *over* him.

She was aware of him shifting in his chair. He never could sit still for long. Then he stood up. *Right, there he goes.* He paced around the room, looking at the art on the walls, picking up objects. She tried to concentrate on the columns of figures, but couldn't help peeking at him out of the corner of her eye.

Those long legs, broad shoulders…

He examined the bowl of flowering succulents she kept on the credenza beneath the window. Then he lifted the framed photo of Frankie and Johnny, her pet cockatoo and her cat. Next to that was a picture of Lucy, her golden retriever. Brett glanced back at the nameplate on her desk, which bore her maiden name. She knew what he was thinking. *Single woman. Her pets are her kids.*

"Did you ever marry?" he asked, confirming her thought.

Hello! She was only thirty-two. Maybe she didn't want to marry. Or maybe she'd kept her own name. She was a career woman, after all. "I'm too busy for a serious relationship."

"You always were smarter than the rest of us." Setting the photo down, he leaned against the credenza, arms loosely crossed. "Tegan begged me for a cockatiel, but I don't like to keep birds in cages."

"I have an aviary—" Renita began, then stopped before she went into a full explanation of how she'd found Frankie as a fledgling with a badly broken wing, and how the vet had said the cockatoo would never fly again. Brett still had a knack for distracting her far too easily.

Clearing her throat, she returned her attention to his business proposal. It appeared straightforward except for one unlabeled column. "Brett, take a look at this set of figures. Are they incoming or outgoing?"

His lanky stride brought him to her desk. "Which column?"

She started to turn the paper toward him, but he moved behind her and leaned over her shoulder, one hand planted on her desk. The heat from his body, the faint scent of aftershave, the long fingers—more distractions. "Uh, that one." She pointed with a manicured nail.

"Right. Okay. That's, um…" He sucked in a breath, clicked his tongue. "Incoming."

"You're sure?" She glanced at him, pushing her glasses farther up her nose. "Because if it's outgoing you may not have even a slim profit."

"I'm sure." He rapped his knuckles on the paper before drawing back. "Incoming. Definitely."

"Okay," she said dubiously, watching him pace back across the room, flexing the fingers of his right hand. She knew that body language; he used to do that when he was nervous before a test at school, when he wasn't certain of his command of the material.

Hmm.

"Okay, *this* is outgoing. Three hundred thousand dollars for refurbishment?" she queried. "That kind of money would buy a lot of paint and carpeting."

"It's for replacing the exercise equipment. Stationary bicycles, treadmills, weight machines—all of it has to go."

"What is that figure based on? I didn't see any costings."

"I didn't have time. It's more like a guesstimate."

"A guesstimate?" she repeated, one eyebrow raised.

"Hey." Smiling, he spread his hands. "Math never was my strong suit."

"You can do better than this."

Even in high school he'd been a big spender, she recalled, financing his nice clothes and fancy car with two part-time jobs. His days in pro football would have made him even more accustomed to having the finest of everything the instant he wanted it. Which was odd, considering he'd come from nothing. His father had been a laborer, his mother an invalid, unable to work. The family had lived in an old cottage on the poorer side of town. His parents still lived there, as far as Renita knew. She was pretty sure his two brothers lived in the area, too.

A few minutes later, she sat back, tapping her pen on the blotter. "You're asking to borrow a total of over a million dollars. That would mean large monthly repayments. It doesn't look to me as if the gym's earnings can cover a mortgage plus the interest on a loan for refurbishment."

"Membership will increase once I spruce up the place."

"Nothing is taken for granted these days. The Community Bank is careful not to let clients get in too deep. Can you put any of your own money into the pot?"

"If I had any, I wouldn't be asking for a loan," Brett said with disarming honesty.

"You don't have savings after thirteen years playing professional football?" Australian Rules footballers didn't make millions, but he'd probably earned a couple grand a year.

"My savings are tied up in a dispute over the divorce settlement," he said. "Once that's resolved I can sink my own money into the business to cut costs. What I'm asking for is more in the nature of a bridging loan."

There was a dispute over the divorce? That hadn't made the papers. Was his ex-wife asking for too much or was he offering too little? This could drag out for years.

"Until your divorce is settled, the amount of money you can contribute is uncertain. It can't have any bearing on my decision." Renita tapped her pen on the folder. "You say you're managing the gym. Do you have any other business experience?"

"None whatsoever," he admitted. "My name will be a draw card. But I won't be resting on my laurels.

I plan to offer state-of-the-art equipment, personal training and fitness classes to cater to everyone. My gym will be small and friendly, with a focus on personal attention. The kind of place where the fitness instructors know the name of every member. Open to whole families, from kids in primary school right up to their grannies."

It sounded good, but at the moment it was still just a pipe dream. "Your name won't be a draw unless you're a visible presence. Will you be hands-on in the running of the business?"

"Absolutely. I'll be there every day, managing the place and giving personal training sessions."

"That's a big time commitment. If you're not used to—"

"I want to do this, Renita." He jumped up and started pacing again. "I *can* do it." He slapped a fist in his palm. "Goddamn it, I *will* do it."

Renita glanced down at the pen between her fingers so as not to be dazzled by his blue eyes. His grit and determination had taken him to glory on the football field. And there was no doubting his sincerity about the gym. Her decisions were based strictly on bank guidelines. She had to be tough. Otherwise, in a small community like Summerside, where she knew almost everyone, she'd be giving away the bank's money right and left.

On the other hand, while Brett's figures were sketchy, it was the only gym in town. And while he lacked management experience, if anyone could turn the business around through sheer willpower, that person was Brett O'Connor.

She glanced up. "Okay, you're in. Barely."

Relief washed over his face. "So you'll approve the loan?"

"I'll authorize the release of funds for you to buy the gym." She punched a few figures into her calculator. "Eight hundred and sixty thousand will cover purchase price plus taxes."

"Excellent. And the new equipment, the refurbishment?"

"I'm sorry. The mortgage is the limit of what the bank will lend you. You haven't provided solid justification for the finances necessary for refurbishment."

"The justification is that members are quitting because the facilities are old and run-down." Frowning, he sat again. "What if I were to cost it all out, itemize every piece of new equipment?"

"I'd be willing to look at it," Renita conceded reluctantly. "But no guarantees, you understand."

His mouth flattened and his nostrils flared as he exhaled forcefully. "You're the boss."

Yes, she was. Renita rose and extended a hand, remembering to suck in her stomach. "I hope your gym will be a huge success."

Brett rose, too, squeezing her hand briefly. He couldn't hide his disappointment. "You'll be hearing from me again soon."

The instant the door closed behind him Renita

undid the buttons of her suit jacket. With a sigh of relief she let her stomach relax. She'd survived their meeting without making a fool of herself. Sure, Brett was dissatisfied with the outcome, but he could hardly expect her to hand him everything he wanted on a plate.

She reached into her drawer for the jar of jelly beans. There was absolutely no reason for her to feel bad.

CHAPTER TWO

FRICKIN' BANKS and their frickin' restrictions. Brett pushed through the double glass doors to the gym. What the hell was he going to do with this shabby old place if he couldn't refurbish it? And what was up with Renita? She never used to be so prickly and standoffish.

"Did you get the loan?" Janet called as he strode through the foyer past the reception desk.

She and Mark, the other fitness instructor, were between classes. They'd already been working here when he'd come on board, and he'd established a rapport with them almost instantly. As he'd explained to Renita, Janet had been juggling managerial duties with her fitness classes. Once Brett had been hired, she'd been more than happy to hand over the reins.

"Talk in a minute." He tossed the manila envelope over the counter toward the desk, but it skidded off and landed on the floor. He kept going, stripping off his jacket without breaking stride.

"Hey, Dad." Tegan brushed back her long, honey-blond hair to wave at him. Her homework was spread over a table in the refreshment area. "Can you help me with geography?"

"Be right back." He took the stairs to the second floor two at a time.

Thank God the men's changing room was empty. The stale odor of sweaty bodies and cleaning products hit Brett's nostrils as the door squeaked open. He flung himself onto a bench and dropped his head in his hands.

Half a loan.

How could he have screwed up on those columns of figures? More to the point, how could he have thought he'd get away with a guesstimate? The answer was simple. Working out the equipment costs had seemed too onerous after everything else he'd done. And if he was honest, he'd thought he could be less rigorous with Renita.

Numbers—they did his head in. He should have asked his brother Tom, a financial analyst with a big firm in the city, for help. Or even gone to an accountant who would have worked up a proper business plan. But Brett had figured that if he was going to run a successful business he ought to know all the ins and outs of the gym's finances. He'd wanted to prove, to himself if no one else, that he wasn't just a dumb jock.

Instead, today he'd confirmed he was no smarter than he'd been in high school.

Renita had always believed in him back then. He felt as if he'd let her down today. Was that why she'd been so reserved, deflecting his attempts to reconnect? What had happened to his funny little buddy? True, they'd lost touch, but at one time they'd been friends. Well, not friends exactly, but they'd known each other. He'd *liked* her, even if they didn't travel in the same circles.

Okay, his comment that she looked fabulous was an exaggeration—she was still overweight. But most women lapped up compliments, especially ones like Renita who probably didn't get many. Why the hell had she taken offense when he'd told her she looked real? That, at least, was true.

"Brett?" Janet banged on the change room door. "Get your butt out here and tell us what's going on, or I'll come in there and haul you out."

"I'm putting on my jockstrap. Want to help?" he called.

"Ooh, yes, please!" Happily married, middle-aged Janet chuckled. A moment later he heard her descending the stairs.

Time to man up. He kicked off his leather loafers and stripped off his shirt and jeans, hanging them up in a locker. He pulled on a navy polo shirt and shorts and went back downstairs.

Stopping at Tegan's table, he dropped a kiss on her forehead. She was wearing too much makeup and her nail polish was a baffling black. Was she really thirteen already? "How's the homework going?"

"Algebra sucks. And I've got this geography assignment." She looked up at him with big eyes. "Can you help me?"

"Sorry, sweetheart, I'm busy with gym stuff right now," he said, pushing aside a stab of guilt. "I've got paperwork to sort out and phone calls to make. Then a personal training session at six."

Tegan sighed heavily and slumped in her chair. "You're *always* too busy with this stupid gym."

"You need to pack up your books, anyway," he added, squeezing her shoulder. "I'll have a quick word with Janet and Mark. Then I'll take you to Grandma and Grandpa's."

Janet was waiting as he approached the reception desk. Though barely five feet tall, she had a muscular build. In her late forties, she could outlast and outpump most of her younger colleagues.

Under her scrutiny, he forced a smile.

Janet gave Mark a high five. "He got the loan."

"Awesome." Mark, an easygoing twenty-five-year-old who towered over Janet, slapped her hand. "That means we've still got a job."

"Unless Brett's going upmarket with the help, too." Janet raised an eyebrow at Brett. "Are you going to hire flash new instructors for your fancy gym?"

"I need you guys more than ever," he replied. "Just don't ask me for a raise right away."

"We'll wait at least a week. Did you get everything you asked for?"

"Pretty much." Brett accepted their congratulations and pats on the back. He wasn't going to talk about what he *didn't* get. Losers were weak. And he wasn't a loser. "Give me a second while I call the real estate agent and tell him to go ahead with the paperwork."

He excused himself and went into the cramped inner office to make his call. His offer had already been accepted subject to approval on the financing. The owner, Grant Springer, was just as keen as Brett for the handover of ownership to take place, and they'd agreed on a thirty-day settlement. It was all happening.

By the time Brett finished the call, Mark had left to teach a pump class and Janet was laminating photocopies of floor exercises for group fitness.

"Almost as good as winning the footy grand final, huh?" she asked over the quiet hum of the machine. Beaming, she nudged him with her elbow.

"Almost," he replied uncomfortably, with a half smile.

She removed a freshly laminated copy. "Was the loans officer impressed with your business plan?"

"She was in awe." Brett was careful to temper his sarcasm.

Janet grabbed the catalog of exercise equipment Brett had been poring over earlier like a kid with a Christmas toy flyer. "Let's start picking out your new goodies."

"Uh, I'll get to that later."

She regarded him with a frown. "Is everything

okay? Yesterday we couldn't tear you away from this brochure."

"Everything's fine. I just have to drop Tegan off at my parents' house for dinner." He reached for his keys and called over his shoulder, "Are you ready, Tegan?"

"Coming." She ambled toward him, the straps of her unbuckled shoes flapping, her school bag slung over her shoulder.

Brett turned back to Janet. "If my six o'clock arrives before I get back, have her warm up on the treadmill. I won't be long."

In his silver E320 Mercedes, Brett cruised down the leafy main street of the village. Tegan chatted about school. Now and then he murmured "yes" or "uh-huh."

"Cool!" Tegan said after one such response. "Thanks, Dad!"

"You're welcome, sweetheart," he replied automatically, then sent her a swift glance. "What did I just say yes to?"

Her eyes widened, all innocence. "Me getting a new dress for the dance."

"You've got dozens of dresses in your closet. Why don't you wear one of those? It's not like anyone in Summerside will have seen them before."

"I only have two party dresses and I've grown out of both of them. Besides, I'm *older* now."

He swiveled to look at her, noticing her developing

figure and the way, sitting side by side, her head now reached his shoulder. "I guess you're right."

The older the girl, the more expensive the dress. He'd learned *that* during his marriage.

Slowing to a halt for the single stoplight in town, he spied the Community Bank on the corner and frowned. Charm had always been his biggest asset, but it hadn't worked with Renita. His efforts to renew their friendship had fallen flat. If that's the way she wanted it, he would stick to business in the future. But he needed his loans manager to be onside to make the gym a success.

His eye fell on a poster erected on the grass verge, advertising the Diabetes Week Fun Run. Renita had been touchy about her father's condition. She was likely worried and feeling helpless, wishing she could do something to fix the problem.

"That's it," Brett muttered. "Two birds with one stone."

He got out his phone and punched in her number at the bank. Her office was the last one on the end, he realized.

"Renita Thatcher." She sounded preoccupied.

"I just wanted to let you know about a special deal the gym is offering," he said, making it up on the spot.

"Brett? Is that you?"

"Two-for-one memberships. I'll throw in five free personal training sessions if you sign up before the end of the week," he added recklessly. She'd *said* she wasn't into exercise, but when people caught the bug they usually came to love the feel-good high of being fit.

"And you think I'm interested because…?"

"Your father is diabetic. I'll bet his doctor has told him to exercise. Does he already belong to a gym in Mornington or Frankston?"

"No," she said. "But he walks his dog, Smedley."

"You and Steve can get fit together. You've got six weeks before the Fun Run—"

"No, no, no," Renita protested. "I told you, I'm not entering the run."

Undeterred, Brett pushed on. "Your dad would be more likely to work out if he had a partner to encourage him, wouldn't he?"

"Brett—" She broke off.

In the silence that followed he could feel her frustration. He thought he understood her reluctance. "Having a personal trainer, you won't have to keep up with all the gym bunnies in a class," he said. "You work at your own pace, with a program tailored to your needs."

"Pushing a little hard, aren't you, Dad?" Tegan murmured from the passenger seat.

Brett motioned to his daughter to be quiet. There was another long pause. *Had* he pushed too hard? Embarrassed Renita? He didn't want to do that.

"It would be good for Dad," she conceded finally. "I'll think about it."

Satisfied, Brett put down his phone and moved

through the green light. "She said she'd think about it," he said to Tegan. But she was really saying yes.

"I'M MISSING THE cricket match on TV," Steve grumbled as Renita dragged him through the doors of the fitness center.

"This won't take long." She hoped not, at least. Gyms were alien territory, bristling with strange machines and hard bodies. And spandex. Oh, God, she could just imagine what she would look like with every blubbery bulge outlined by spandex.

But she had to admit Brett was right—her father needed a concrete goal in his quest to improve his health. "If the place looks good you can become a member and sign up for the Fun Run."

Steve balked on the black mat just inside the foyer, blinking at the bright lights and loud music. "I'm no runner."

"You don't want another hospital episode."

"I don't want a stroke, either." His slacks sagged at the back and his shirt buttons strained over his barrel-shaped belly. Behind his steel-framed glasses, his brown eyes revealed his reluctance.

"That's why you're going to get fit *before* the event," Renita coaxed. "When I was a kid, who told me I could do anything I set my mind to? Now *I'm* telling *you* you can do it. I know you can."

"There's no one here," Steve said, glancing at the reception desk, with its scuffed lime-green paint. "Let's go."

"Shh, listen." Renita could hear Brett talking on the phone in an office behind the desk. "Let's wait a minute."

The faint odors of perspiration and rubber floor mats conjured up the discomfort and small humiliations of high school gym class. Chafing thighs, sweaty clothes, being picked last for every team...

Renita moved farther into the building, taking in the gym's poor state of repair. Paint was chipped on the corners of the pillars, the linoleum flooring was worn, and Out of Order signs hung from several of the exercise machines. Brett would have his work cut out for him, turning the facility into the fitness center of his dreams.

"This is a dive," Steve muttered, echoing her thoughts. "Why'd you bring me here?"

"Because my bank is lending money to the new owner." Knowing her dad kept a keen eye out for a bargain, she added cannily, "Plus there's a sale on memberships."

"I get enough exercise walking Smedley." Steve removed his glasses and polished them on the hem of his shirt, drawing Renita's attention to his round stomach.

"You've been walking for weeks now and haven't lost an inch off that gut of yours," Renita said. "That trip to the hospital was a wake-up call. You need to change your habits."

In the multipurpose exercise room to their left a female fitness instructor was barking out encouragement to a perspiring middle-aged man doing sumo squats. "See, Dad, that could be you."

"In that case, let me outta here. If we leave now I can still catch the last of the cricket." He spun and headed for the exit, surprisingly nimble despite his bulk.

Renita grabbed his arm. "Oh, no, you don't."

"Can I help you?" Brett, wearing a navy polo shirt sporting the gym's logo, emerged from the office. "Hey, Renita. G'day, Mr. Thatcher. Steve, isn't it? Nice to see you again."

"Brett O'Connor?" Steve turned to Renita with a frown. "You didn't tell me this was *Brett's* gym."

"Didn't I?" She deliberately hadn't mentioned Brett by name, worried that it would deter Steve, even though he was a rabid footy fan and a supporter of Brett's old team, the Collingwood Magpies.

"Welcome to the gym." Brett extended a hand to Steve, nodding to Renita. "I'm pleased you're taking me up on the two-for-one gym membership."

"Dad's interested, not me." She stepped back and nudged her father forward.

He threw her a startled glance. "But you said—"

"I said I *might*." Okay, so she'd fibbed a little to get him to come. It was for his own good. While she was happy to persuade her dad to sign up, it didn't mean *she* was going to join. Sure, she needed to lose weight, but she had no desire to sweat and puff, especially around Brett.

"I'm not joining unless you do," he protested.

"Do you follow football, Steve?" Brett said casually, leaning against the counter.

"Of course." Almost grudgingly, he asked, "How do you like Collingwood's chances for the cup this year?"

Brett rattled off a bunch of football statistics and tossed around names, drawing Steve deeper into conversation. Renita's dad bought it hook, line and sinker, even reciting Brett's own stats to him. As if the conceited ass didn't recall every goal he'd kicked. If her father still harbored a grudge for the sporting hero, he wasn't showing it.

"Which was your high point?" Steve asked. "The year your team won the Grand Final or when you were awarded the Brownlow Medal?"

"I ought to say the Grand Final, but if I'm honest, it was winning the Brownlow."

"I don't blame you. Top honor," Steve said gruffly. "How's that knee of yours?"

"I had surgery on it last year. It's fine unless I work it too hard." Brett took a clipboard from the counter and passed it to him, along with a pen. "If you'd like to write down your name and contact details we can send you more information. No obligation, of course. What type of membership would suit you best—yearly, monthly or a ten-visit pass?"

Steve scribbled his name and phone number. "What's the best deal?"

"Yearly," Brett said. "But if you take out a trial

three-month membership, and later want to convert to annual, we'll do a pro rata."

"The three-month trial sounds good." Steve handed back the clipboard.

Brett tried to pass it on to Renita. "We have a two-for-one special, remember?"

"I told you, working out isn't my thing."

"Come on, Renita," Steve urged. "We could split the cost."

"Yeah, come on, Renita," Brett echoed, a twinkle in his eyes.

How dare he tease her? *Those days are over, pal.*

"How about a tour of the facilities?" she replied. "I'd like to see what the bank is investing its money in."

He gazed at her for a beat. "All right."

He led them across to the cardio room, where stepping and rowing machines, elliptical trainers, reclining bicycles and treadmills stood empty. Brett flicked one of the Out of Order signs. "I plan on replacing all these machines as soon as I can get the financing."

"That sounds good, doesn't it, Renita?" Steve said.

"Sounds expensive."

Next to cardio were glass-fronted squash courts, also not in use. Across the way was the multipurpose room. "That's Janet, one of our fitness instructors, giving a personal training session."

Brett moved into the weight-training room. Two

men were working with free weights while a woman sweated it out on a machine. "All these will be replaced, too. Tea and coffee over there," he went on, indicating three small tables with seating for about twelve. "I plan to put in a cappuccino machine."

"It does appeal," Renita murmured.

"Plus fresh carrot juice for a healthy alternative," Brett added. He started up the central flight of stairs, toward the source of loud music and thumping feet. "Here on the second floor we have the aerobics room. We'll add to the range of classes as demand grows, so there'll be something to suit everyone."

Renita followed, leaving Steve breathing hard, to bring up the rear. The door to the aerobics room was shut, so she looked over a half wall into the far squash court, which had been turned into a spin class room.

"I'll be replacing all those bikes, too. And putting a new office in over here," he added, drawing her attention to an unused space beneath a window at the front of the building.

He had confidence to burn, she'd give him that.

Steve made it to the top of the stairs and slumped onto a padded exercise bench.

"You okay, Dad?" Renita asked. He nodded, blotting his forehead with the back of his hand. She turned to Brett. "He would have to take it easy to start."

"We tailor training to the individual. There's also a low impact seniors class." Brett glanced back at her.

"There's plenty for the younger crowd, too. Sure you don't want to join?"

"She'll join." Steve leaned forward, elbows on his knees, trying to catch his breath.

"No, Dad, I…" Renita stopped, not wanting to argue with her father in public.

"I'll be downstairs if you two want a moment." Brett ran down the steps, leaving them alone.

She sat beside her father on the bench.

"Renita, honey, you were right. I've been fooling myself that walking is enough. Climbing up those stairs just now…" Steve wiped more beads of perspiration from his forehead. "I need more exercise. But I don't want to do it alone."

"The last time I worked out was in high school, and that was under duress," she argued. "A gym is my worst nightmare. Maybe I could do the Fun Run with you. We could walk if we had to."

"Ten miles is a long way for us couch potatoes, even walking." He peered at her from behind his half-fogged glasses.

Renita dropped her gaze. Her mum was busy with her yoga classes and meditation. Jack—her brother—had his hands full running the local Men's Shed volunteer group and manufacturing the GPS he'd invented for small aircraft. Her sister—well, Lexie was an artist, so absorbed in her portrait painting that she could barely manage her own life. It would have to be up to Renita to help their father.

And what about her own health? If she didn't start

moving, she'd just get fatter and fatter, to the point where she'd have real problems like her dad. Was that the future this brainiac was creating for herself?

"Okay, we'll do it together." She gave him a hug, and his arms tightened around her, his jaw raspy against her cheek. "Let's go tell Mr. Superstar."

Downstairs, they found Brett putting away free weights in the exercise room.

"We'd both like to join," Renita said. "And have the two-for-one deal with a personal trainer."

"Excellent." Brett hefted a pair of twenty-five-pound dumbbells as if they were feathers, and placed them in the rack. "I'll take you both on myself, if you're game."

Lifting her chin, Renita said, "Bring it on."

BRETT LOADED FATHER AND daughter up with time-tables, newsletters and receipts. He made arrangements for Renita to bring Steve to his first training session the next morning.

"I'll see you for yours Friday afternoon," he told her, holding the door open for them as they went out.

"Way to go, boss." Janet congratulated him when she returned to the reception desk after her session was over. "Two new members."

"It was touch and go there for a while." Brett pulled up a window on the computer screen and started to enter their details.

"I saw you work your magic. Never a moment of

doubt." Janet slanted him a quizzical glance. "Who's the woman?"

"Renita Thatcher. She's the loans manager at the bank. I knew her in high school."

"I thought I caught an undercurrent," Janet said. "Were you two an item?"

"God, no," Brett said, saving the page. "She tutored me in math."

Half a dozen women from the aerobics class drifted down the stairs, chatting and laughing. On the way out, the single ones all sent flirtatious glances at Brett. He was friendly, but ignored the unspoken invitations. The small number of people in the class was a worry. There should have been twenty, at least.

"You could have your pick of that bunch," Janet observed when the door shut behind the last one.

"I don't date clients." He began to shut down the computer.

"Probably wise." Janet pulled out the equipment brochure again. "These machines are really expensive," she said, flipping through the pages. "You could get better deals buying used ones through the internet."

Now was the time to mention that his loan wouldn't even cover cheap used equipment. But Brett found he just…couldn't.

"I wouldn't waste my time. These babies are top of the line," he said, reaching for the brochure. "It's time I started making a list and checking it twice."

He wanted the best equipment money could buy. He'd find that money, somehow. He'd never gotten anywhere in life by being cautious.

CHAPTER THREE

"Fun Run. Isn't that a contradiction in terms?" Renita said to Lexie as they wandered through the mall, shopping for exercise clothing. "I mean, what's fun about sweating?"

"Ask Jack—he's the athletic one in the family. It's to do with endorphins." Lexie pushed back her long, unruly blond hair with paint-stained fingers. Her naturally slender build, coupled with the fact that she regularly forgot to eat when she was working on a portrait, meant she never had to worry about her weight. "You should take up yoga."

"My body doesn't bend properly. My stomach gets in the way." Renita stepped sideways to allow a young mum pushing a stroller to get by. She scanned ahead, past clusters of teenagers and middle-aged couples, for the athletic store her assistant, Poppy, had recommended.

"I can't believe you actually got Dad to agree to run," Lexie said. "I don't think I've ever seen him in shorts, let alone moving faster than a walk."

"He only signed up because the great Brett O'Connor talked him into it." Renita rolled her eyes.

"Brett O'Connor?" Lexie repeated. "Wasn't he the footy player you were madly in love with in high school?"

"Mild infatuation," Renita corrected, hoping her sister wouldn't recall how she'd doodled Brett's name in every notebook. Ah, here was the shop. She stopped in front of the display window. "I *love* the color of that sports bra."

"Cobalt-blue. Perfect with your dark hair," Lexie declared. "Try it on."

"And expose my midriff?" She made a face. "No thanks."

"All you've bought so far are three oversize T-shirts and a pair of baggy shorts," Lexie complained. "Do it."

"I'm so fat. It'll look horrible on me."

"You're pleasingly plump."

"Who am I pleasing? Not me." She eyed her reflection in the window critically. She didn't hate her body; she just didn't love it. "I need to lose twenty pounds."

"You're *going* to. As soon as you start exercising. First you need the proper gear."

"I guess there's no harm in trying it on. It doesn't mean I have to buy it." Renita went into the shop. Flicking through the clothes rack, she found her size in the sports bra. "Hold these," she said, and handed Lexie her shopping bags before finding an empty fitting room.

"What did you see in him, anyway?" her sister

asked, taking a seat outside the cubicle, bags rustling. "Jocks aren't your type."

"Tell me about it." Renita's voice was muffled as she pulled her scoop-necked ivory top over her head.

"Was it because he was unattainable?"

"Who wants a guy who's unattainable?" Renita was much more pragmatic than that. And yet the reason she'd liked him didn't have anything to do with practicality. "He made me laugh." She sighed. "And he was hot."

"He *was* gorgeous," Lexie agreed. "Still is, I'll bet."

Oh, he is. "It's funny, though," Renita said. "Beneath all that cockiness, I don't believe he's as sure of himself as he pretends."

She stared at herself in the mirror, eyeing the bulge of flesh below her bra strap, the roll above the waistband of her slacks, then turned away.

"Was it fun catching up on old high school stuff with Brett?" Lexie asked.

"Not much to catch up on," Renita replied, taking the sports bra off the hanger. "After I stopped tutoring him I hardly ever saw him again."

"Didn't you ask him to a dance and he turned you down? I seem to remember you sobbing to me over the phone about it. When I was living in Melbourne, going to art school."

"I did ask him out. He said no. No great loss. As for me sobbing over Brett O'Connor? No way." That last bit was a lie but Renita didn't want to revisit the past. She'd moved on since then, had her share of boyfriends…her share of disappointments in love. Brett had no power to hurt her anymore.

She tugged on the sports bra, sucking in her gut as she turned sideways to check the fit in the mirror. The cobalt-blue did look great, but oh, that midriff. And her breasts were too small. If she had a bigger bust maybe her stomach wouldn't look so huge.

She tried to imagine a slimmer version of herself. Was it possible? Could she work that hard, lose that much weight? For years she'd been in denial, telling herself she wasn't *that* heavy, concealing her girth with flattering garments. What would it feel like to wear a revealing top and look trim and toned?

Suddenly, she wanted to find out.

"Are you done?" Lexie called. "I'm dying for a coffee."

"Just a minute." Renita dragged the bra over her head and changed back into her clothes. She opened the door to the cubicle. "As soon as I pay for this."

"Awesome!" Lexie said. "I'm so proud of you for having the guts to wear something revealing."

"Oh, I'm not going to *wear* it," Renita said. "It's going to hang on the back of my bedroom door. Every time I look at it, it'll be incentive for me to keep exercising."

"You go, girl."

"Then when I'm buff, Brett will want me just as

badly as I once wanted him. I'm going to look so hot he'll slip on his own drool."

"No great loss, you say?" Lexie commented drily.

Renita ignored that and moved to the checkout. "He won't be able to have me. *I'll* be unattainable."

"Renita, don't be a tease," her sister said, following behind. "Okay, he hurt your feelings in high school, but you can't hold that against him now. He seems like a nice guy. Even the gossip magazines could never find any sleaze on him."

"Brett's a big boy." Renita tossed her ponytail. "He can take care of himself."

"It's not just him I'm worried about," Lexie said. "You're not as tough as you pretend."

"I *am* tough." Renita's fists tightened around the plastic hanger. If she was going to be around Brett she would have to develop a hide like a rhino.

"HEY, GRANT." Brett shifted the phone to his other ear while he gave change to a gym member for the coffee machine. "The financing is all approved, the sale is going ahead. I just wanted to confirm that my salary as manager continues up until the date of the transfer of property. Then I'll be on my own." He chuckled as Grant offered commiserations. "I'm looking forward to taking over. Can't wait, in fact. If you happen to be in town for the grand opening, be sure to come by. I'll let you know when it is."

Brett hung up and made calls to a few painting

companies and flooring installers. He didn't have a loan for refurbishment—yet—but there was no harm in getting a few quotes so he'd be ready to roll when he did get the money.

He glanced at his watch. Nearly 6:00 p.m. He needed to get Tegan from his parents' house, where she was helping babysit his brother Ryan's little girl.

He left the reception desk to poke his head into the weight room, where Mark was wiping down the seats and handles of the machines. "I'm taking off now," he told him. "I'll be back in an hour or so. I'll close tonight."

"Sure thing, Brett." Mark lifted the bottle of spray cleaner. "Catch you later."

On his way to his parents' he stopped off at home to pick up a glass coffee table he had no use for. When he'd split from Amber she'd kept the mansion on the Yarra River and bought all new furniture, giving him the old pieces. He knew his mum and dad would be thrilled to get a nearly new coffee table in perfect condition.

A half hour later he pulled into the gravel driveway of the seventies timber cottage where he had grown up. The ramshackle building, added onto in hodgepodge fashion as the family grew, was tucked in an old subdivision of Summerside. The backyard was big enough for a chicken coop, a veggie garden and, when Brett was a kid, for him and his brothers, Ryan and Tom, to chuck around a football. In his big earning years Brett had tried to buy his parents a newer house, but they'd wanted to stay where they had space for the grandkids to play. From the sounds of laughter over the fence, Tegan and little Charlotte were bouncing on the trampoline.

His dad opened the front door, big and bluff as ever. Hal's graying hair still held traces of blond and his shoulders were as wide as his son's. "Hey, Brett." He feinted a karate chop.

Brett parried, only to find himself gripped in a headlock. He hooked a leg around his father's ankle and got him off balance long enough to break away. Hal immediately twisted his arm up his back with an evil chuckle.

"Uncle!" Brett cried, knowing that otherwise this could go on for twenty minutes or more. Hal released him and he shook his shoulders to relax them. "Geez, Dad, when are you going to take up golf?"

"Golf is for sissies. Mary!" Hal bellowed down the hall. "Brett's here."

His mum, short and slight, limped forward slowly, hampered by her prosthetic leg. Brett went to meet her, picking her up and enveloping her in a bear hug.

"Let me go," she cried, flustered and laughing, pushing back her curly auburn hair. After she was safely set back down, she said, "Are you and Tegan staying for dinner?"

"I have to get back to the gym in an hour. I'm just

dropping off that coffee table we talked about. Dad, want to give me a hand?"

Hal followed him out to the car and helped him unhook the bungee cord holding down the trunk of the Mercedes. "How's it going at the gym?"

"I got the loan. In thirty days the business will be mine." Brett slid one end of the thick glass out of the trunk over the padding, steadying it so his father could grab hold. When Hal had removed the glass, Brett bent his knees and hefted the marble base, grunting under its weight.

"And the bad news?" Hal asked, somehow hearing it in the tone of Brett's voice. He balanced the heavy piece of glass on his hip and crunched over the gravel to the front door.

"It's all good." Brett shifted the marble to get a stronger grip, then went sideways into the house. "Where do you want this?"

"Over here." Mary waved him to a spot in the cozy living room in front of the his-and-hers recliners in worn brown Naugahyde.

"Brett's got himself a fitness center," Hal told his wife.

"That's wonderful." She motioned them a little farther to the right. "Not too close to the fireplace."

Brett lowered the base, then helped position the glass top. Merlin, the fluffy gray cat, came to inspect the new addition to his home. Mary hunted up a cloth and a bottle of window cleaner.

"I'll go find Tegan," Hal said, leaving his wife to do the final touches.

"Thank you, Brett. This table is lovely." Mary began to polish the glass top. "Doesn't that girl who tutored you in math in high school work in the loans department? I'll bet it helped that you knew her."

Brett picked up Merlin and stroked him until he purred. "Oddly enough, needing math tutorials was no recommendation for a business loan in Renita's eyes."

"Renita, that's her name." His mum straightened, pressing a hand to the small of her back. "But what do you mean, no recommendation. Didn't you get what you wanted?"

Somehow his mother always managed to coax information from him that he couldn't tell his father. "Not the full loan," he said flatly. "I can buy the gym but not refurbish it."

Hal came through the door from the kitchen. "The girls are coming in now."

"Tell your father," Mary said to Brett. She took a potted African violet off the windowsill and placed it in the center of the table.

Hal glanced from her to Brett. "What is it?"

Brett groaned. "Don't, Mum…."

"Brett's got a problem with the bank. They won't give him enough money. Can we help?"

"No, I'll be fine," Brett said firmly. His parents' meager savings would see them through retirement as long as nothing unexpected came up. He didn't like asking for help from anyone, and he definitely wouldn't take it from his folks, who had so little to spare.

"Have you talked to Ryan or Tom?" Mary asked.

"No, and I'm not going to. They both have families and expenses of their own."

"What about taking in a silent partner?" Hal suggested. "One of your old footy mates."

Brett rubbed his jaw. It wasn't a bad idea. Some of the guys could afford to throw a couple hundred grand his way as an investment. But to ask would mean revealing his ongoing problems with Amber and his financial embarrassment. "Nah, I'll think of something."

Hal clapped a hand on his shoulder. "Course you will."

"If you change your mind, you come to us," Mary said.

"Thanks," Brett said, knowing he never would.

"Bring Renita around for dinner sometime," she added.

"We don't see each other socially."

"Not even as friends?" Mary asked. "I always thought you had a soft spot for her."

"I don't know why you'd think that." He kissed his mother's cheek. "I'll get Tegan on my way out."

"Stay for dinner," Mary said. "I was expecting you to. Ryan and Emma are coming soon to pick up Charlotte."

Tegan appeared in the doorway, cheeks flushed, her ponytail coming loose. "Please, Dad?"

Four-year-old Charlotte, her light brown curls bouncing, ran up and pressed her hands together. "Pweeze, Unca Brett?"

Brett laughed. "Okay. But I'll have to eat and run. Renita and her father joined the gym. She's coming in tonight for her first training session."

RENITA WARILY EYED THE racks of variously sized dumbbells lining the walls of the exercise room like instruments of torture. Loud music pumped from speakers in the corners of the ceiling. All by herself, she stood awkwardly, waiting for Brett. She felt like the first person to arrive at a party.

Through the glass wall she could see a girl in the local high school uniform of green gingham dress and white kneesocks doing her homework in the refreshment area. In the adjoining room, a faux blonde gym bunny with a spray-on tan pulled the handles of an exercise machine, flaunting her taut abs and sculpted body.

Renita hated her.

She wanted to *be* her.

Mirrored walls on three sides reflected Renita's lumpy body, mostly hidden beneath an oversize T-shirt and baggy gym shorts. She hadn't even lifted a dumbbell and already she was perspiring, just thinking about the embarrassment of working out in front of Brett. Her vow to Lexie seemed ludicrous now. What had she been thinking?

She was going through this for her father's sake, Renita reminded herself. Steve was counting on her. Closing her eyes, she breathed deeply and slowly, trying for some of the inner peace her mother found through meditation.

It didn't matter how weak Renita was on the inside, as long as she appeared to be strong on the outside. Brett could be as sexy and charming as he liked. It would be like water off a duck's back.

Renita breathed deeply one more time. Ready, she opened her eyes. Brett was nowhere in sight.

She might as well do something while she waited, so she rolled an exercise ball off its stand, glancing around to see if anyone was watching. No one was paying attention. She sat on it, crossed her arms over her chest and leaned back to do a crunch the way she'd seen on TV. Back, back…

"Hey, Renita." Brett came through the door, clipboard in hand.

She lost her balance, sliding sideways as the ball rolled out from under her. Arms and legs flailing, she hit the floor.

"You okay?" Brett asked, offering her a helping hand.

Cheeks burning, Renita ignored it and scrambled to her feet. She promptly tripped over the wide soles of her new running shoes. "I'm f-fine."

"We'll get to the Swiss balls later," he said. "First,

we'll test your fitness level—cardiovascular, strength and flexibility."

Renita brushed off her shorts, pushed up her glasses and tightened her ponytail. "Right."

She happened to glance in the mirror. And barely stifled a groan. Brett was a Greek god—blond hair, strong jaw, broad shoulders, tanned muscular arms and legs. Confronted by their reflections side by side, she found the facts inescapable.

He was hot. She was not.

Brett O'Connor ever begging her for a date? Not likely. She couldn't believe she'd thought for a second she could make him want her.

"Can you give me ten push-ups?"

"Knees or toes?" she asked, as she lowered herself to the mat. Toes—*ha!* As if.

"Knees will be fine."

She positioned her hands, took a breath and started to lower her torso to the floor.

"Keep your butt down, back straight," Brett ordered.

A strand of hair fell in front of her glasses. Her arms wobbled. She got within a few inches of the floor and began to push herself back up, shoulder muscles straining.

One down, nine to go.

Five—her biceps started to burn. Six—her arms were shaking. Seven—her butt was high in the air—to hell with proper form. Eight—as she lowered herself, her arms gave out.

"Oof." She fell flat on her chest and face, glasses knocked awry.

She glanced around, mortified in case anyone had seen her collapse. The only person watching was the teenage girl doing her homework in the coffee area—probably waiting for her mother or father to finish working out.

"I'll have to work up to ten," Renita muttered, dragging herself to her knees. Brett offered her a hand again, and she once more ignored it, using a bench to pull herself to her feet. "How am I doing? Be honest."

"You're not the *most* out-of-shape person I've trained—"

"Thank God for that."

"But close." There was a twinkle in his eye.

"What's next?" she growled, hating him.

"Sit-ups. Do as many as you can in sixty seconds."

Back down she went, clumsily dropping onto her butt, then stretching out on her back. Ah, this was nice. Restful.

"Whenever you're ready," Brett said.

"Oh. Right." She linked her fingers behind her head and used her stomach muscles to pull herself up. Again and again. As the seconds ticked by she got slower and slower. Never had a minute seemed so long.

Finally Brett said, "Stop."

She collapsed on her back and shut her eyes.

"Enough." Maybe if she played dead he would go away.

Brett crouched in front of her. "Renita? Time for the treadmill."

She opened one eye and peered at him through fogged glasses. "It's no use. I can't do this. Dad'll just have to train for the Fun Run on his own."

"I never figured you for the type that gives up," he said. "But if you're that much of a wuss you'd probably stop running after a couple of blocks. That wouldn't be much help to your father. Just as well you pack it in now, before you get Steve's hopes up."

She struggled to a seated position and took off her glasses, furiously polishing away the fog with her shirt hem. "I know what you're doing. You're trying to get me angry so it'll stiffen my resolve. Well, even if the spirit is willing, the flesh—" she grabbed a double handful of her belly through her T-shirt "—is too damn weak."

"Okay, I admit I was trying to use reverse psychology to motivate you," he said. "But I learned that from you."

"Me?" she said. "What are you talking about?"

"Trigonometry. Calculus. I wanted to throw in the towel more than once during our tutorials. You told me, sure, I could give up studying. It wouldn't make any difference if I failed the exam, because everyone knew you didn't need brains to play football."

"Oh, yeah, I remember." Amazing that she'd

had the nerve to be tough with someone she worshipped.

"I want you to know that your technique worked. I could tell that you believed in me." He laughed. "Probably the only one who did."

"But…" She cast her mind back. "I thought you failed math."

"I did. But I had an offer from the Collingwood football team at the end of grade eleven. My parents were going to let me sign up. I decided to finish high school instead."

She hadn't thought he could surprise her. He wasn't just a footy-obsessed jock. Apparently he possessed an ounce or two of academic discipline. "I wasn't aware of the football offer. That was gutsy of you to turn it down."

"I may have failed math, but you did teach me something." His gaze lifted to hers, his eyes unshuttered. "To go after what I wanted and stick to it until I got it."

CHAPTER FOUR

NO, NO, NO, NO. She wasn't that easy.

Renita shoved aside the warm and fuzzy feelings that befuddled her when Brett looked into her eyes.

"Reverse psychology might have worked in high school, but I'm a grown woman." She climbed to her feet again. "Too smart to fall for lame motivational tricks."

"I wasn't trying to trick you." Brett rose fluidly, his manner brisk. "Let me give it to you straight. Exercise is damn hard work, especially when you're not used to it. Give yourself a chance. The benefits will be worth it."

Renita wiped off her upper lip, put her smudged glasses back on and sipped from her water bottle.

Was she going to storm out of here because she couldn't handle chafing thighs and lactic acid burn in her muscles? If Brett had pushed on with his schoolwork when everything was against him, she wasn't going to back down from a physical challenge.

"All right," she said. "What's next?"

"I was going to get you on the treadmill but you can have a breather." He flipped a page on his clipboard. "Instead we'll take your baseline stats so we can monitor your progress in the coming weeks. Let's head over to the scales."

"Scales?" Renita's courage flagged again. "You mean…?"

"We measure your weight," he said matter-of-factly. "And your height. Also bust, waist and hip circumference. Calf, upper arm, thigh…"

She stopped listening. The mortification she'd experienced in high school was nothing compared to the horror of standing on the scales with Brett O'Connor recording her weight.

Her air sole running shoes felt as heavy as moon boots as she followed him out of the cardio room and over to the upright tape measure in the open space next to the refreshment area. The girl with the blond ponytail glanced up from her books again. Great, now Renita had an audience of two.

Brett measured her height first. No problem there. She was five foot six. He confirmed it and wrote the number in his loopy scrawl on her sheet.

Renita knew what was coming next and could feel her face growing hot. She prayed for some emergency, like a fire in the building or an earthquake.

"Hop on the scales. Don't be shy," Brett said, either unaware of her embarrassment or ignoring it. "Everyone goes through the process."

Not even she knew exactly how much she weighed, or the circumference of her waist.

The phone rang in reception. Brett disregarded it, waiting for her to get on the scales.

"Shouldn't you get that, Dad?" the schoolgirl said when the phone kept ringing.

Finally he noticed the empty desk. "Hang on, I'll be back in a minute," he said to Renita. Setting the clipboard on top of a filing cabinet, he walked off.

Renita released her breath. She wiped away the perspiration trickling down her temple.

"I'll finish measuring you," the girl said, getting up.

"That's nice of you."

"Not really. As soon as he's done with you he can take me home." The girl's eyes were the same deep blue as Brett's. Her fresh young skin was dusted with powder and blush, and her lips were shiny with pink gloss.

"You called him Dad," Renita said. "Are you Tegan?"

"How do you know my name?"

"Brett told me about you yesterday when he came to my bank for a loan. I'm Renita."

Tegan glanced toward reception. "He could come back any minute."

"Right." Renita stepped on the scales. She forced herself to look at the digital readout. It was worse than she thought.

"Guys are clueless sometimes," Tegan said, busily writing. "Even my dad." She picked up a tape measure and, motioning for Renita to lift her arms, stood on tiptoes to slide it around her bust. Again she noted the number. When Tegan moved to measure her waist, Renita sucked in her stomach.

"I wouldn't do that if I were you," the teen said. "It'll just take longer before you show a loss. Anyway, once the measurements are entered on the sheet he doesn't look at them."

"Are you certain?"

"Positive," Tegan assured her. "Not even for the real hotties."

"Thanks," Renita replied drily. But she relaxed, even adding a little extra girth by pushing out her stomach.

Tegan glanced up. "Cheater."

Renita laughed sheepishly and glanced over to reception. Brett was writing something down. "It looks as if he's winding up the call."

"We're almost done." Tegan took the last few measurements. "What were you guys talking about?"

"When do you mean?" Renita said, confused as to why the girl was asking.

"After your situps," Tegan explained as she entered the last numbers on the sheet. "I just wondered, because he jokes around a lot, but he doesn't usually have conversations with his clients."

"He was just giving me a pep talk." Renita changed the subject. "What homework are you doing?"

"Math." Tegan made a face. "I suck at it so bad."

"Just like your father."

"What do you mean?"

"You'll have to ask him." Renita nodded at the sheet of measurements and smiled. "Thanks, Tegan. We girls have to stick together."

The teen held up her hands. "I only helped you because I want my dad to finish quickly."

"I didn't mean anything by it," Renita said, surprised by the undercurrent of antagonism. "Is there a problem?"

"Women are always trying to get to my dad by cozying up to me. I'm sick of it."

"I'm not interested in your father," Renita protested.

Tegan's wry expression was cynical beyond her years. "That's what they all say."

AFTER DINNER BRETT SET UP his laptop in the breakfast nook. At the other end of the table, the *Beginners Book for Sailors* was held open to a page on knot tying by strands of soft white rope Tegan was supposed to be using to practice.

Instead she was Wii dancing in the adjacent family room, gyrating her narrow hips in time to pop music as she followed the movements of the figure on the TV screen.

"Tegan, have you studied your knots for this week's lesson?"

"Not yet. Can you do them with me?"

"After I finish this." Brett opened a new spreadsheet and labeled the first column Item. Beneath that he typed in "Exercise Bike." Then he started a new column, Unit Cost, and plugged in "$5,995." Quantity "6." Punching the numbers into his calculator, he came up with a figure that he entered into the column labeled Total Cost.

He sat back and frowned. It wasn't the total cost. That wouldn't come until he'd added up all the rows with their individual items. He scrolled back to Unit Cost and changed it to Unit Price, then altered Total Cost to just plain Cost.

Tegan missed a step and the dance game ended. As the next program loaded she wandered over to the table and leaned against his shoulder to peer at his laptop. "Whatcha doing?"

"Costing out new gym equipment." He typed in "Elliptical Cross Trainer," Unit Price "$8,795," Quantity "6." He calculated, then double-checked. This time Renita wouldn't catch him out on a single mistake. "How are the sailing lessons going?"

"I get all wet and the salt spray wrecks my hair."

"You're lucky. I never had the opportunity to take sailing lessons when I was a kid."

Tegan picked up the ropes and studied the diagram, making a halfhearted attempt to work a bowline before tossing the rope aside. "I have a partner for the sailing dinghy. Her name's Amy."

"Is Amy a friend at school?"

"She's in my grade." Sighing heavily, Tegan tried the knot again. "Who was that woman you were training today at the gym? Renita someone."

Brett glanced up. "Renita Thatcher, the loans manager at the bank."

Tegan planted her elbows on the table to undo the knot. "Do you like her?"

"Sure, I like her. I like everyone." Brett consulted the equipment catalog for the StairMasters and entered the unit price. Tegan was still there, studying him. "What now?"

"You were different with her. Not…flirty and fake, but just, I don't know…different."

He winced. "I act *fake* with women?"

"Not always. Just with gym bunnies and football groupies."

"Oh, them." Brett was tired of women who gushed over him because he used to be a professional football player. By comparison, Renita's prickly standoffishness was a breath of fresh air. "I knew Renita in high school."

Tegan started working another knot. "Was she your girlfriend?"

"She tutored me in math."

"Ah, so that's what she meant."

"Sorry?" Brett murmured, deep in the middle of a calculation.

"I told her I hated math and she said, 'Just like your father.' Were you really crap at it?"

"Yes, I was crap at it." Pointedly, he added, "But *you* don't have to be, not if you study."

Tegan frowned at the granny knot in her hands and double-checked the diagram in the book. "Did you look at the notice I brought home asking for chaperones for the junior high school dance? Will you do it?"

"Sure." Brett lost track of which number he'd entered into the calculator. "Wait a minute. What did I agree to now?"

Tegan repeated what she'd said.

He rubbed a hand through his hair, bemused. She had a habit of asking him things when he wasn't really listening. Sometimes he wondered if she did it on purpose. "Okay, I'll chaperone."

"Good." A run of musical notes signaled the Wii was ready for the next dance game. Tegan tossed the rope down and ran back to the other room.

He began to go over his calculations one more time. He punched in the last few numbers and came up with a grand total of $235,000.

It was a lot less than the three hundred grand he'd asked for. Surely Renita couldn't say no again. He thought about her training session. As at their meeting at the bank, she'd avoided talking about personal matters. Well, fine. If that's the way she wanted it. This time when they met, he'd be all business.

RENITA WINCED WITH every step as she slowly crossed the lawn to the aviary. Even her neck was sore. Her golden retriever, Lucy, padded faithfully at her heel.

"*Squawk!* Hello!" Frankie lifted his yellow crest

and slid his claws back and forth on the bare tree branch that was his perch. "Wheeere's Johnny?"

Johnny, the calico cat, was curled up asleep beneath the huge shady leaves of an oyster plant. Hearing his name, he opened almond-shaped green eyes and yawned.

Renita stooped to stroke the cat's gold-and-gray fur, then straightened painfully. In a way, Brett's assumption had been correct—her pets were her kids. Their needs were simple and they gave her utter devotion. She would like to have children someday, but for now she lavished her affection on Frankie, Johnny and Lucy.

She went to the garden shed for a scoop of bird seed and poured the mixture into the feeder, careful not to get any chaff on her suit. The cockatoo dipped his head for a mouthful of sunflower seeds and cracked them open. Renita ran a finger down the bird's snowy wing feathers. With luck he would live for another fifty years and she'd be showing him to her grandchildren.

"Renita, are you home?" Hetty's spiky gray head appeared over the side gate. She lifted the latch and came through, loose-limbed and graceful in her flowing pants and tunic.

Steve shuffled slowly behind in a plaid shirt and dark trousers, every movement eliciting a wince and a scowl from him. Lucy got up and went to greet them, nudging Steve's hand for a pat, recognizing her pal, the dog lover.

"Dad, you look as sore as I feel," Renita said.

"Never mind that. Have you seen Smedley? He's missing." Steve's sparse hair was ruffled, his face flushed and perspiring. "He hasn't turned up here, has he?"

"No, why would he do that?" Renita replaced the scoop in the bin and shut the door to the garden shed.

"Yes, why would he come to Renita's house?" Hetty said impatiently. "She lives across town from our place."

"I need to cover all bases," Steve said, mopping his perspiring face with a handkerchief. "Man, it's hot."

"Are you okay?" Renita asked. "You didn't walk here, did you?"

"We've already been all over Summerside by car," Hetty explained. "That wasn't good enough. Now we have to go over the same route on foot."

"He could have been hit by a car and thrown into the grass by the side of the road," Steve said.

"You always look for the worst-case scenario," Hetty complained. "He'll turn up eventually."

"You see?" Steve muttered to Renita. "She doesn't give a damn what happens to my dog."

"Of course I care." Hetty's small hands tightened around the loose folds of her pants. "I'm traipsing all over the neighborhood, aren't I?"

"Sit down for a while." Renita led the way to the

deck chairs on the patio. "I need to leave for work soon, but I'll get you a cold drink."

"Thanks," Hetty said. "Your father could use a rest."

"I'm not an invalid," Steve snapped. "I'm training for a Fun Run. If I can't walk a few miles I'll be in big trouble on the day of the race."

"Still, you should have a drink of water before you carry on," Renita said.

"We can only stay for a minute," he grumbled. "If I sit too long I'm liable to seize up completely." He sank onto the cushions with a sigh.

As Renita filled glasses with ice and water she glanced at her parents through the window over the sink. Although they sat side by side, they looked away from each other, not speaking. A crisis should have brought them together, but it seemed to have had the opposite effect.

She carried the tray of drinks outside. "How did he get out?" she asked, trying to diffuse the tension.

"He dug beneath the fence," Steve told her. "He never did anything like that before I went into the hospital. If your mother had been home where she was supposed to be, instead of gallivanting—"

"I was at a spiritual retreat." Hetty's voice had a gritty edge. "If *you* hadn't eaten yourself into a diabetic coma—"

Renita's cell rang from the kitchen, where she'd left it. "Excuse me," she said, and ran back inside to answer it. "Hello?"

"Poppy here. Brett O'Connor called. He wants to know if you have time to see him today. I wouldn't have called you at home, but since it's Brett…"

Renita rolled her eyes. "I can probably squeeze him in first thing this morning. I'll be there shortly."

She hung up and went back to her parents. "I've got to go to work. Can I drive you somewhere?"

Hetty finished her water and put the glass back on the tray. "Thanks, Renita. You can drop me off at home."

"I'm going to walk along the beach," Steve said in a gruff voice. "The little fella loves chasing waves."

"It's too far," Hetty protested. "Don't you agree, Renita?"

"I've got to find my dog."

"Never mind the ride, Renita," her mum said in a long-suffering tone. "I'll have to go with him."

Renita walked them to the street. "Let me know if you find Smedley."

She went back inside to finish getting ready for work. As she applied a light coat of mascara, she pondered the best way to handle Brett. At the bank she'd been too businesslike. At her personal training session she'd felt too vulnerable—though she wasn't sure he'd noticed. They were going to meet regularly; there was no escaping it. She needed to find a middle ground, neither too familiar nor too cool.

She should chat a bit, she decided, the way he'd tried to with her. His daughter would be a neutral topic. Every parent liked to talk about their kid.

IN THE BANK LOBBY, Brett sat with his ankle crossed over his knee, foot jiggling. He tapped the arms of the chair, caught Renita's assistant watching him covertly, and smiled automatically. She blushed as scarlet as her lipstick and ducked back behind her computer screen, blond bob swinging.

Tapping the manila envelope against his thigh, he checked his watch. The assistant—Poppy, her nameplate said—had told him Renita would be in soon. Since then, twenty minutes had passed. Where was she?

Another minute went by. The line of customers in front of the tellers inched forward. At least *they* were getting somewhere.

He jumped to his feet, paced the dark blue carpet, slapping the envelope against his thigh. This morning one of the gym's regulars had canceled his membership. Added to the three already lost last week, the gym was losing members twice as fast as new ones were joining.

"Good morning, Brett," Renita said from behind him.

He whirled around. "Morning."

He breathed in her fragrance, something fresh and floral, as she walked past him to unlock her office door. He noted her full, curvy figure molded into a tight-fitting suit, and her dark, wavy hair loosely pinned up.

What the hell? What was he doing, checking out Renita? Today was strictly about business.

Brett waited for her to take a seat behind her desk before he sat. She lowered herself slowly, with a barely disguised grimace.

"Feeling sore after your workout?" he asked.

"A touch," she admitted.

"The best cure for stiffness is more exercise."

"Naturally," she said drily. "Torture is its own reward."

Slowly she readied her desk for the day, putting her purse in a drawer, stacking loose papers over to one side. A jar of jelly beans sat next to the phone. With a glance at him, she started to reach for them, then drew her arm back, wincing.

"Don't put them away on my account," Brett said. "I like the black ones myself."

"You'd have to fight me for them. Since you'd win, they're going in my drawer." Setting her jaw, she half stood and leaned over to grab the jar. "On second thought, I'm throwing them out. If I'm going to kill myself with exercise, there's no point undermining my efforts." She dropped the jar into the rubbish bin with a loud metallic clank.

Next she tried to shrug out of her jacket, but her movements were constricted and obviously painful.

Brett hesitated, then finally jumped up and went around her desk. "Let me." He eased it off her shoulders. From his vantage point he could see the V in her blouse and the shadow between her breasts.

Geez, he was doing it again. Shut down the radar, mate. This is Renita.

"You might like a hot bath," he said, moving back to his chair.

A blush washed over her cheeks.

"I mean for sore muscles. Or benzocaine ointment."

"Right," she said briskly, clearing her throat. "So, what's up?"

Brett removed his spreadsheet from the envelope. "I've itemized and costed the equipment I need. I think you'll find everything's correct this time."

Renita took the papers. "You got onto this quickly."

"I need to move on the refurbishment." Brett clapped his hands on his knees, forcing himself to sit still.

Instead of looking over the document, she leaned back in her chair. "How are your parents doing?"

"They're good." Silence. She was waiting for more. "They're…in the same house I grew up in, doing the same things they've done for the past thirty years. Dad's retired, but he still teaches karate. Mum has her garden club. They play bowls every weekend. Same old, same old."

"I think that's nice. My parents don't do much together anymore. Tegan's a lovely girl. How old is she?"

Oh, for God's sake. *Now* she wanted to chat? "Thirteen. In grade eight."

"Is she enjoying school? Aside from math, that is."

"She's doing okay. It's been an adjustment for her,

transferring so close to the end of the school year."
He eyed his spreadsheet pointedly. "So…"

"I notice she hangs around the gym a lot. Has
she made new friends yet? Gotten involved in school
activities?"

Brett stifled a sigh. If Renita wanted to talk, he
would have to go along with it. "She's taking sailing
lessons at the local beach club. Her partner, Amy, is a
friend from school." He paused. "She's excited about
her junior school dance, which apparently I have to
chaperone."

"A school dance. Fun." Renita's eyes dropped to
the spreadsheet.

Finally, Brett thought.

Her pen tracked line by line as her gaze moved
down the sheet of costings. Brett watched her closely,
trying to gauge her reaction. She looked interested,
thoughtful. Her eyebrows arched ever so slightly.

She put her pen down and looked up. "You've been
very thorough."

He shrugged, hiding a swell of pride. "No big
deal."

"But…" Renita perused the document, pen tapping
the desk blotter. "Does the equipment have to be
brand-new? Couldn't you get by with cheaper machines? I had a look online and there's a lot of used
exercise equipment out there."

"You don't know what problems you're getting
when you buy used," Brett explained. "This particu-
lar brand is state of the art. I want to be ahead of

my competitors in Frankston and Mornington, not playing catch-up."

"But do you have to replace all the equipment at once?" she persisted. "Why not spread the cost over time?"

"Unless I refurbish properly, I won't get the influx of new members I need to make a profit."

"I hear what you're saying, but this is a large amount of money."

"It's a business. There are set-up costs."

"I'm sorry, Brett. I can't approve this loan. But I will authorize you to receive $50,000. Perhaps in six months—"

He sat back, stunned. "I don't have six months." He couldn't believe she was turning him down. Again. "If I'm going to get the gym off to a good start I need to act quickly."

"I understand your urgency and I'm sympathetic. If you can just be patient—"

Brett surged to his feet and began to pace her office. "I know the fitness industry. Fifty thousand is chicken feed. You can't tell me when and where I can spend money on my business."

"See, that's the thing, Brett…." She waited a beat. "I can."

He turned around, eyes narrowed. Was she enjoying this?

"You'll be able to paint and put new flooring in, as well as buy some secondhand equipment to replace the broken machines. Does that make sense?"

"I already have used equipment. I want brand-new." Hell, now he sounded like little Charlotte, begging "Unca Brett" to stay for dinner. "I can turn the business around. I *know* I can. But only if I have the funds to do it."

"I'd like to give you the whole amount, Brett, I really would. But I can't."

"Can't or won't?"

"It comes to the same thing."

"This will be the *Brett O'Connor* Fitness Center." He jabbed her desk with a finger. "I have a reputation to live up to."

"And I have to abide by bank guidelines." She spread her hands. "Fifty thousand. Take it or leave it."

Brett paced away. Belatedly, he recalled how her smile had evaporated when he'd mentioned Tegan's dance. And why, that first time he'd come to the bank, her lame excuse about why she'd dropped his tutorials in high school hadn't rung true. "Is this because—"

"Because…?"

"No, it can't be." He shook his head.

"What?" she asked.

"Because of what happened in high school before our grade eleven dance?"

He'd let her down gently but even so embarrassment had blared from her crimson face like a stuck car horn. Poor kid. He'd forgotten all about the incident until now.

"Please, give me some credit as a professional." Her manner stiff, she rose and started gathering his papers together. "I'll draw up the necessary documents and have my assistant contact you when they're ready."

"I apologize. That was a dumb thing to say. Could we grab a coffee and talk about this?" This was no attempt to charm. Just sheer desperation.

"There's nothing to talk about. Anyway, I have another appointment." She handed him his envelope, then came out from behind the desk, walked over to the door and opened it.

Burning at her dismissal, Brett followed. He'd spent hours on this. She'd rejected his hard work after looking at it for five minutes. "Fifty thousand is pointless."

"You don't have to take it."

"Oh, I'll take it," he said bitterly. "I have no other choice, as you keep reminding me."

"You'll see I'm right, Brett. As the gym picks up you can buy new equipment piece by piece."

"No problem." Slapping the envelope against his thigh, he turned and strode out the door. With or without her help, he was going to get what he needed for his gym.

CHAPTER FIVE

RENITA'S STOMACH GRUMBLED as she walked along the winding path above the creek, stepping over tree roots and pushing back hanging branches. Her breakfast of fruit and yogurt had been three hours ago. Instead of concentrating on searching for poor lost Smedley, she was fantasizing about bacon cheeseburgers and pepperoni pizza.

The searchers were strung out along the path. Jack's booming voice carried across the deep ravine, calling Smedley's name. Steve whistled the three-note tune that usually had the Jack Russell terrier bounding toward him. Sienna, her red hair standing out against the green foliage, combed the terrain between Jack and Steve.

Oliver, Sienna's fourteen-year-old son, took off after Jack's dog Bogie along the rabbit trails that ran steeply down to the creek. Lexie trailed in the rear, gathering wildflowers, as often as not looking up into the treetops as into the bushes.

Renita's thoughts drifted back to food. Fresh sourdough bread slathered in warm Brie cheese… No, no, no. No more bread or chocolate or cheeseburgers.

In spite of all her exercise her weight had gone up. Muscle gain? Still, her pants felt a little looser.

She wondered if Brett had noticed. Not that she cared what he thought. How dare he suggest she'd withheld the loan as payback for him rejecting her in high school. Her revenge would be more subtle. And much more personal. She was going to look so hot that he wouldn't be able to keep his hands off her. She wanted him to want her the way she'd once wanted him.

A tiny part of her still wanted him, if she was honest.

But Brett was just as out-of-bounds as the bacon and eggs she could smell frying in one of the houses that backed onto the creek.

Jack stopped suddenly, his head tilted, a hand cupped behind his ear. "Did you hear that? It sounded like Smedley growling."

Renita came to a halt, listening. Birds twittered among the gum leaves. Children's voices called from backyards. Somewhere, a lawn mower disturbed the Saturday morning calm.

"I don't hear anything." She breathed in deeply. Onions—there were onions frying, too.

"There it goes again," Jack said.

"That's my stomach."

Jack groaned. "Didn't you eat breakfast?"

"Hours ago!"

He pulled an energy bar out of his shirt pocket. "Here."

Renita salivated over the fruit-and-nut bar. But she knew exactly how many calories it contained—the equivalent of a whole meal under her new regime. "Thanks, but no."

"I'll have it," Lexie said, catching up with them. She tore open the wrapper. "Renita's on a diet."

"Way to go, Lexie. I was keeping it a secret in case I don't lose any weight."

"It's only Jack." Her sister bit into the bar.

"What's only Jack?" Sienna had retraced her steps to see what the family confab was about.

With a sigh, Renita explained. Sienna was a doctor, after all. Probably she should have consulted her before starting her extreme diet and exercise program.

"I thought you looked thinner." Sienna's green eyes studied her in the light filtered through the gum trees.

"It's since you joined the gym," Jack said to Renita. "I've always told you exercise was the key."

"Yeah, yeah," she grumbled. "You've been waiting for years to say I told you so."

They resumed walking, Jack moving ahead to catch up to Steve and Oliver. Lexie waded into the bushes to pick a drooping white peony from a plant that was growing wild.

Sienna fell in beside Renita. "What prompted the lifestyle change?"

"I'm trying to help Dad get fit," Renita explained.

Sienna was Steve's doctor. "We joined the gym to-gether and we've signed up for the Fun Run."

"Jack and I have tried to get Steve to run with us," Sienna said. "He always makes an excuse."

"He knows you two would outstrip him," Renita said. "Whereas I'll slog along at a snail's pace with-out making him look bad." She paused while they navigated in single file around a fallen tree. "I also want to be healthier."

She'd tried dieting before, but every time, she'd lost a few pounds, then gone back to her old habits of eating too much and exercising too little.

"And you're doing it to get Brett," Lexie said, tuck-ing the peony into her bouquet.

"Lexie!" Renita glared at her sister over her shoul-der. "I don't know what she's talking about. How are the wedding plans going, Sienna?"

"Since Jack and I have both been married before, we didn't want a white wedding. We're going to have the ceremony in Bali, just us and Oliver. It'll be ro-mantic, in a tropical garden with a waterfall." At Renita's clear disappointment, she added, "But first we'll have a party here so everyone can celebrate with us."

After they'd talked about Bali and the wedding, Lexie tried to turn the conversation back to Brett. Renita cut her off. "Where's Hetty today? When I asked Dad where she was, he just muttered and turned away."

"She told me she's fed up looking for the dog,"

Lexie said above a double armful of flowers. "She thinks Dad should accept that Smedley's gone, and try to find peace."

"He'll never give up hope unless—" Renita broke off. *Unless they found a body.*

Her thought seemed to hang in the still warm air, killing conversation. They'd walked a few minutes in silence when a shout came from down by the creek.

"That's Oliver," Sienna said, quickening her steps.

The teenager burst out of the bushes. "I found him!"

Renita hurried after Sienna. Steve broke into a lumbering jog. Lexie threw down her flowers and hiked up her long skirt to run.

"Where is he?" Steve peered through the bushes and the tangle of trees overgrown with vines. "Is Smedley all right?"

"H-he's having a fit." Oliver bent at the waist, panting, his curly blond hair falling over his forehead. "I tried to pick him up, but I couldn't hold him. His legs are going crazy. Like he's trying to run but can't. He's lying on his side, shaking and twitching."

A bloodcurdling sound, half crazed bark, half canine scream, pierced the still air.

"Smedley!" Steve's face contorted and his hands clenched.

The tortured bark was followed by another. Renita felt the blood drain from her face. Jack took off down the path through the bush, Sienna and Lexie close on his heels.

Renita put an arm around her father, supporting him as he staggered, holding him back when he would have lurched down the ravine after the others. "Wait here, Dad. Jack will bring Smedley out. He'll be all right."

Her heart clutched as the sound of Smedley's agony rang out. She prayed she was right.

BRETT SHUT THE DOOR to his bedroom so Tegan couldn't overhear his conversation. Taking out his cell phone, he punched in Amber's number. He ought to go through their lawyers, but that would take too long.

"Amber," he said when she picked up.

"What is it, Brett? I'm out for lunch. Make it quick."

He could hear the sounds of restaurant clatter and conversation in the background. "How long it takes is up to you," he said, controlling a surge of irritation. "We're not making progress with the divorce agreement. Until we settle, neither of us has access to the bulk of the money."

"Hang on." A moment later the sounds of dining receded. "All you have to do is give me what I want."

"I've already been more than generous, which even your lawyer admits." Brett paced through the sliding doors onto the balcony. "Be reasonable."

"*You* got custody of Tegan."

"Yes, but you see her whenever you want." That was one of the few things they'd agreed on. Even so, Amber was so busy that Tegan didn't spend as much time with her mother as she would have liked. "And now you want an even higher percentage of my assets."

"*Our* assets, Brett."

He could just imagine her inspecting her nail polish as she said it. "You were a manicurist. You didn't bring any material assets of your own, and you didn't work after we married."

"If you think being on the board of the Friends of Children's Hospital isn't work, then it's obvious you've never done it. You try cold-calling people, asking for money."

"I'm doing it right now."

"Yeah, well, I'm a pussycat compared to the captains of industry I have to suck up to."

There were a lot of things Brett could have said, but he refrained. For all Amber's faults she worked her guts out to raise money for research into the rare blood disorder her sister's six-year-old son suffered from.

But Amber had also acquired a taste for luxury from their years of living the high life. And she seemed determined to get every penny out of him she could.

He sucked in a deep breath, then blew out slowly.

"Will you please consider my latest offer and get back to me as soon as possible? It's very important."

"Why?" she asked, suddenly suspicious. "What's your hurry? The interim agreement gives us both enough for day-to-day expenses."

"I'm trying to start a business," he explained, pacing back inside the bedroom. "The bank won't loan me the full amount I need."

"So you're over a barrel, huh?" Amber said thoughtfully.

"Not really." He became wary too late. "Amber—"

"It's simple, Brett. As soon as you agree to my terms you'll be good to go."

Damn. He should have known better than to give her the slightest leverage. "I don't understand why you're being so greedy when you're living with another highly paid football player."

There was a long pause. "Jarrod and I broke up."

"Oh. Sorry." *Not.*

"I don't expect any sympathy from you. But I'm on my own now. And yes, I've gotten used to a certain lifestyle. When Tegan comes to stay we like to go out and do things."

"Shop, you mean."

"I refuse to go back to doing nails." Amber sulked. "It pays peanuts."

"As if you'd have to go back to work. My offer is more than—"

"Dad?" Tegan knocked at his door.

"Hang on a minute," he said into the receiver. "What is it?"

His daughter poked her head inside the room. "Are you talking to Mum? I thought I heard you say 'Amber.'"

"Yes." He went back to his ex-wife. "Tegan's right here. Do you want to talk to her?"

"Of course I do. Put her on."

Brett handed the phone to Tegan. She walked out of his room and down the carpeted hall, talking animatedly about the coming weekend, when she'd stay at Amber's apartment. Naturally, shopping featured prominently.

Brett stalked back out to the balcony. Now that Amber knew how badly he wanted the money, she was going to be even more difficult about the settlement. There was no point going back to the bank and asking Renita for a third time. There had to be another way.

WEARILY, RENITA PUSHED through the glass doors of the gym for her training session. She was tired and strung out from sitting with her father at Smedley's side last night until the veterinarian clinic had closed.

The smell of fresh paint hit her as she walked through the gym doors. Tarps covered the floor. A man in splattered white overalls wielding a long brush was rolling on fresh cream-colored paint across the ceiling of the weight room. Brett was talking to a second painter mixing up a bright blue in the open space adjacent to the refreshment area.

Janet, behind the desk, held the scanner to beep Renita's membership card. "Brett won't be long. Why don't you warm up on the treadmill?"

"All right." She found her chart with her personalized program in the filing cabinet next to reception, and made her way to the cardio room. Climbing onto an empty treadmill, she punched in the program Brett had given her and started walking.

Exercise was the last thing she felt like doing, so she adjusted the treadmill program to a low level of intensity. She ambled along, her gaze flicking between the digital readout of calories burned— ridiculously low—and the wall-mounted TV tuned to a talk show.

"Hey, Renita," Brett said, coming up beside her machine. "Let's ramp this up." Without waiting for her to agree, he pushed some buttons.

"Hey!" Renita tripped, recovered and was forced into a jog. "It's too fast."

"You can do it. You need to push yourself."

She tried to keep up, she really did. Two minutes into the new pace she felt her feet slipping out from under her. She shot her hands out and hit the big red Stop button.

As the treadmill slowed she dragged her fogged glasses off and glared at him. "I can't *do* it."

"Sorry," he said, sounding anything but.

She grabbed her water bottle and her towel. "I didn't think you'd be one to hold a grudge."

She stalked out of the cardio room, consulting her chart as she entered the exercise room. Tegan, working on her laptop in the refreshment area, glanced up as she passed, but Renita didn't pause or say hello. Grabbing a pair of five pound dumbbells off the rack, she began doing biceps curls.

Brett took his time joining her. He watched her do ten curls, then barked, "Another rep. Keep your abs tight."

Renita gritted her teeth and started on the next ten. "I've had a terrible night, O'Connor. I don't need any flack from you."

"Yeah, well, you're not the only person who has problems." He ticked off a column on her chart. "And just for the record, I don't hold a grudge. After I left your office that day I came back here and socked the punching bag and worked out for a couple of hours."

"Did it help?"

"Exercise always helps. It just doesn't change anything."

Renita struggled through another ten curls. "Maybe it's not a good idea for us to work together. I'd like Janet to take over my training."

"No," he said baldly, meeting her gaze and staring her down. "I took you on. I'm not going to stop just because we had a conflict outside the gym. Give me some credit for being professional," he added, throwing her words back at her.

She lifted her chin. "Fine, then. Do your worst."

Renita should have known not to issue Brett a challenge. He worked her twice as hard as usual, giving her double the reps that were on her chart. She did everything he asked, determined not to let him call her weak. At the end of the hour her clothes were soaked through with sweat and her arms and legs were limp.

She sank onto a bench and dropped her elbows on her knees.

Brett started to walk away. Then he came back and stood over her. "Are you okay?"

"I'm fine," she mumbled. "Just go away."

"What's wrong?"

"I'm *fine.*"

"So you say. How's Steve? You guys missed his training session yesterday."

Renita burst into the tears she'd been holding back for nearly twenty-four hours. "Smedley is really sick. We found him down by the creek. It was awful."

"Smedley?"

"My dad's dog, a beautiful little Jack Russell terrier."

"Hell." Brett hesitated, then sat on the bench beside her. Tentatively, he put his arm around her shoulders. "What happened to him? Is he…will he live?"

Renita resisted the urge to lean against Brett and take comfort from his solid warmth. She'd seen him touch lots of clients, male and female—a pat on the back, a squeeze of the shoulder. It was friendly, meant nothing. She had to stop being so hyperaware of him. "We don't know anything yet. I'm meeting Dad at the vet clinic later."

"Let me know how it turns out." Brett hugged her close, then dropped his own elbows on his knees. "I had a run-in with my ex-wife last night."

"Amber?" Renita didn't know whether she should say anything, but she couldn't help being curious. "Was it about…money? Is she ready to come to an agreement?"

"It's always about money with her. And no, she's not ready to settle."

"What does she want?" When he hesitated, Renita added, "I'm asking as your loan officer. I have an interest in the outcome of your divorce." And if he believed that…

"I was willing to split fifty-fifty with her. She wants three-quarters of the estate."

"That doesn't seem fair."

"It's not. She does a lot of charity work, but that's not the reason. She's scared because she lost her meal ticket and she never bothered to learn to do anything except paint nails for a living." Brett rose and held out a hand to help Renita up.

She accepted, wincing as her legs complained about the workout she'd just gone through.

"I was hard on you today," he said.

"You were a slave driver. All you needed was a galley whip and I could have rowed to Mesopotamia."

He cracked a smile. Grudgingly, she gave him one back.

"Next time we'll get you and Steve out jogging," Brett said. "Outdoors. Three miles."

"No way. I'm not ready for that. I need to be in better shape to run." *In public.* She couldn't think of anything more humiliating than jiggling and wobbling her way through the streets of Summerside.

"If you're serious about the Fun Run you need to start training." He glanced at the clock. "Gotta go. Pump class."

She watched him take the stairs two at a time. "We're going to talk about this!"

"He's in a bad mood today," Tegan said from behind her.

Renita turned and, through smudged glasses, saw the girl watching her over the screen of her laptop. "I noticed." She walked over to fill her drink bottle from the water cooler, nodding at the laptop. "You get a lot of homework."

"No homework today," Tegan said, busily clicking through web pages. "I'm looking for a dress for the school dance."

Renita sipped her water standing behind Tegan's chair so she could watch as the girl scrolled through the selections. "I like the blue one."

"Dad would never let me wear anything cut so low."

"It *is* a bit revealing."

"I can't wait until I'm in grade eleven and can get a proper prom dress." Tegan clicked onto another website. "What did you wear to your prom?"

"I didn't go."

Tegan glanced up. "Why not?"

Renita leaned back, sipped her water. "No one asked me."

The teen looked baffled. "Couldn't you have asked someone?"

"I did, but…" She hesitated. It felt weird to be telling this to Brett's child. "He said no."

"That must have sucked."

"It did," Renita admitted. Still did, even now, when she thought of herself sitting home alone that night, knowing Brett was out with someone else. "Do you have a date?"

"Dad says I'm too young to date." Tegan's cheeks turned pink. "There's a guy I like…."

"What's his name?" Renita said in a teasing voice.

Tegan's blush deepened. "Oliver."

Renita sat up straighter. "Oliver Maxwell?"

"Do you know him?" Tegan tried not to appear eager.

"His mother, Sienna, is marrying my brother, Jack. Oliver will be my stepnephew. He seems like a really nice boy. Does he like you?"

"I *think* he does." Tegan dropped her chin in her

hands and smiled dreamily. "I hope he asks me to dance."

"If he doesn't, you ask him. Don't be shy."

"What if he says no? I'd die."

Renita looked at Tegan, who was blonde, pretty and sweet. She couldn't imagine any boy turning her down. "He'll be flattered. But let me give you a tip. Find the right moment, when he's on his own. That way neither of you will be embarrassed if he says no for whatever reason."

"Got it," Tegan said, nodding.

Renita hesitated. "Is your dad taking a date?"

"I doubt it. He doesn't have a girlfriend right now."

"That's kind of surprising, isn't it?" She hoped Tegan wouldn't notice she was blatantly fishing for information.

"He could have dozens of dates, if he wanted. Women email photos of themselves wearing bikinis or in their underwear or even wearing nothing at all. It's disgusting."

"I tend to agree."

"I don't *want* him to have a girlfriend," Tegan added with a swift glance at Renita. "He hardly has any time to spend with me as it is."

It was impossible to miss the warning. If only Tegan knew how little chance there was of she and Brett getting together. "You wouldn't want him to be lonely."

"He's got *me*." The girl spoke with defiance, but

then her voice cracked, betraying a note of uncertainty that was heartbreaking.

RENITA DODGED an agitated poodle trying to paw off his bucket collar, and approached the forty-something brunette at the vet clinic reception. "Is Steve Thatcher here? His dog, Smedley, came in last night."

"They're in the treatment room." The receptionist rose and ushered Renita through a door and past a row of empty animal cages.

Renita pushed open the door she gestured to, and went inside. Her heart sank when she found Smedley, unconscious, laid out on a trolley lined with a towel. An intravenous drip fed in through a needle inserted into a shaved patch on his leg.

At least he was alive.

"Hey, Dad," Renita said softly. "How's the boy?"

"Hanging on." Steve's jaw was gray with stubble and his wrinkled clothes were the same ones he'd worn yesterday. He straightened, a hand pressed to the small of his back.

Renita walked over to gently stroke the brown-and-white spotted fur on Smedley's neck. The only sign of life was the slight rise and fall of his rib cage. "Did the vet figure out what's wrong with him?"

"David reckons Smedley ate fox bait."

"Fox bait." *Poison.* "He will recover, though, won't he?" Renita searched her father's face anxiously.

Steve shrugged, his mouth working as he stroked Smedley's front paw over and over with one fingertip.

"It's still touch and go. The little bugger is tough but…" He cleared his throat. "The vet assistant will be along soon to turn him."

Renita gazed at the animal. Even in sleep the little terrier was never this still; he was always twitching, chasing rabbits in his dreams. "Is he in a coma?"

"He's anesthetized. The drip is saline laced with sodium bicarb. It could take up to twenty-four hours before he shows signs of recovery."

Renita heard the unspoken *if.*

"Have you had dinner?" she asked. Her dad looked at her blankly. "You didn't even have lunch, did you?" She rose. "Okay, you're coming with me. We're going to eat."

"I don't want to leave him."

"You're not going to do him any good by becoming sick yourself."

Steve pushed his glasses up to rub his bleary eyes. "Gotta admit…I have a hankering for fish and chips."

The thought of hot, salty chips made Renita's mouth water. "Or we could get something less fattening."

"To hell with the diet," Steve growled. "I'm hungry."

Renita led the way out through the clinic to the parking lot and her car. "You look thinner. How much weight have you lost?"

"Eight pounds."

"That is *so* not fair. Men lose weight more easily than women," she complained, only half joking.

"I have more to lose," Steve groused, rubbing his belly.

At the takeout in the village Steve ordered battered fish and a large order of chips. Renita decided to be strong and got grilled fish, no chips. When the food was ready they carried it to a picnic table in the park. She tore open the butcher's paper wrapping. Steam billowed from the hot fish and crisp wedges of potato.

Instead of diving in, Steve curled his fists on the picnic table. His face, already haggard from losing sleep over his dog, drooped, his jowls settling into folds.

Renita covered his hand with hers. "Smedley will be all right."

"It's not that." His voice was thick, his eyes misty behind his wire-rimmed glasses. "I been eatin' dinner with Hetty every night for forty years."

"Let's call her, ask her to join us." Renita squeezed his hand. "She'd want an update on Smedley."

"She doesn't care about my dog."

"You're wrong, Dad. At any rate, she cares about *you*. You shouldn't take Smedley's sickness out on her." Renita reached in her purse for her phone. "It'll be fun to have a picnic—"

Steve's gnarled fingers shot out to still her hand. "She's gone."

"What?" Renita said, not understanding. "Gone where?"

"Back to Queensland. Left this morning."

"Oh, no." Renita dropped her phone back in her purse. She poked the plastic fork into her grilled fish and discovered she'd lost her appetite. "How long will she be away?"

Steve took a handkerchief from his pocket and blew his nose. "She didn't say."

Renita shoved a fried potato into her mouth. Briefly, she registered the crispy texture and salty taste. Mindlessly, she took another. "She can't just keep running off like that," Renita said, chewing furiously. "What are you supposed to do?"

"Just get on with things, I suppose." His hand shook as he lifted another bite to his mouth.

Seeing her father so upset scared her. Renita wanted to shake some life into him. He'd lost weight, but it was more like he'd lost substance. "But she just comes and goes as she pleases. It's not right. What sort of marriage is that? Call her. Tell her to come home."

"I've got to take care of Smedley. One thing at a time."

"You can't drop everything for the dog. You missed a training session yesterday."

Steve shrugged. "I'll make it up. Sometime."

Renita looked down at her greasy fingers and felt sick. After a week of strict dieting, she'd eaten half a dozen French fries without thinking. "Speaking of training…do you remember when I was a teenager and I used to tutor Brett?"

"Sure. Why?" Steve handed her a paper napkin.

"I'm curious. Why didn't you like him?" She hadn't given it a thought for years, but now that Brett was back in her life she wanted to know.

"He wasn't your type."

"Wasn't my type," she repeated. Brett had said the very same thing. "Do you mean I wasn't pretty enough for him? Not popular enough?"

"You were good enough for any boy. Still are."

"Then did you think *he* wasn't good enough for *me?*"

"I just didn't like him hanging around the house all the time."

"We were studying."

"I saw the way he looked at you. Like a wild dog eyeing a young lamb."

Renita's mouth twisted in a skeptical grimace. "Come on, Dad. He was out of my league."

"Then maybe it was the way *you* looked at *him*. The fact is, he was trouble," Steve growled.

"Trouble in what way?" she persisted. "He was always polite to you and Mother."

"The boy was sexually active," Steve said bluntly. "You were too young for that kind of nonsense. Which is also why I wasn't going to discuss it with you."

Renita dropped her plastic fork and sat back, stunned. Sexually active. In hindsight she didn't doubt Brett had been, although she'd been too naive to realize it at the time. "Wait a minute. How did you know he was sexually active?"

"He was good-looking, popular. There were rumors about him and the girls he went out with. I didn't want him corrupting you."

Whereas she would have loved to have been corrupted by Brett O'Connor. Okay, maybe fifteen was too young to have sex, despite what went on in schools these days. But she would have liked to have had the opportunity to say no.

Steve rose and tossed the rubbish into the bin next to the barbecues. "I have to get back to the clinic."

Renita slowly wrapped the remains of her meal in the crumpled paper. Even after more than a decade, the thought of Brett seducing her in high school made her tingle. *Would* she, innocent and awkward and in awe of the handsome jock, have said no?

Maybe. Maybe not.

And if he wanted to make love to her *now?*

CHAPTER SIX

RENITA LEANED CLOSE to the mirror in the optometrist's office, breath held, getting ready to stick her finger in her eye. For the fifth time. The first contact lens had gone in straightaway. The second was proving trickier.

"That's right." The assistant, a young woman with red hair and black rectangular glasses, added encouragingly, "Just touch the contact lens to your pupil…."

Renita felt the lens slide off onto her eyeball. She blinked, her vision blurry. Blinked again and it cleared. She looked around the shop, amazed that the clarity was even better than with her glasses. "I can't wait to try them out at the gym. It'll be so nice not to have my glasses fog up every time I start to sweat."

"Oh, we have antifogging solution," the assistant said. "Would you like to try that?"

"No, I'm happy with the contacts."

Renita glanced at her reflection in the mirror. Her eyes had always been her best feature. Why hadn't she gotten contact lenses years ago?

Minutes later she stepped out onto the street, feeling almost naked without plastic frames on her face. Different. Lighter. More attractive. This was great. Not only could she see better, she looked better.

Her cell phone rang. Renita stepped to the edge of the sidewalk between the butcher and the green grocer to answer it. "Hey, Lexie. What's up?"

"Can you meet Jack and me at the pub tonight?" Her sister sounded teary. "We need to have a family conference about Mother and Dad."

"I saw Dad yesterday. He's pretty depressed about her being away and Smedley and everything."

"It's worse," Lexie said with a shuddering sigh. "I talked to her this morning."

BRETT SIPPED HIS BEER in a corner of the Summerside pub while an old high school buddy and his wife chatted about their little boy. After he'd put Tegan on the train for Amber's apartment in the city, he'd arranged an evening out to catch up.

"Tony just turned one year old," Bree said, sipping gin and tonic. "He's almost walking, isn't he, hon?"

"Another week, I reckon," Danny agreed, swirling his draft beer. "I've already bought him his first football."

"I'm happy for you guys." Brett clinked glasses with his friend.

"There's Jack Thatcher," Danny said, nodding toward the door. "He's a mate of yours, isn't he? My neighbor belongs to his volunteer organization, the Men's Shed."

Brett glanced over his shoulder as Jack, Renita and Lexie walked into the pub and took seats by the window. They hadn't seen him. In fact, they didn't seem to notice anyone. The trio appeared awfully somber for a Saturday night.

Renita looked different. She was wearing jeans and a sleeveless silk blouse, and he could tell she'd lost a bit of weight. She didn't look too bad, really. Something else about her had changed, but he couldn't put his finger on it. Her wavy hair fell loosely around her shoulders instead of being tied back. But that wasn't it.

"Danny, look at the time. We've got to go," Bree said, glancing at her watch. "Sorry, Brett. The sitter can only stay till eleven."

"No worries. It was great to see you both."

Danny drained his beer. "We'll have you and Tegan over for a barbecue soon. Bring your swimsuits."

"Look forward to it," Brett said, half rising to say goodbye. "Drop into the gym sometime."

After Danny and Bree left, Brett's gaze drifted back to Renita. She leaned over her glass of wine, speaking earnestly to Jack and Lexie. Once or twice she touched her fingers to her eyes as if she was blotting tears.

Had Steve's dog died? Renita, like her father, had always loved animals. She'd always been emotional, too, as he recalled. Lexie and Jack weren't crying, but they looked upset.

Brett drained his beer. He might as well have an early night. Rising, he wove among the tables toward the exit. With luck he could slip past without being seen. He didn't want to intrude on what was clearly a family conference.

Then Jack happened to glance up. "Hey, Brett."

Brett had no choice but to walk over. He included all three in his greeting. "How's everyone?"

"Fine. Have a seat," Jack said.

"I don't want to interrupt. I was just leaving—"

"No, stay." Lexie scraped her chair over so he could pull up another between her and Renita. "We're done with the family stuff."

Brett glanced at Renita, eyebrows raised.

"Please. Join us," she said stiffly.

This was awkward. Yes, he was tired of women fawning over him, but Renita was looking at him like something the cat dragged in. Still, he didn't have much choice now but to stay, so he brought another chair over and draped his jacket on the back. "What are you all drinking? I'll get another round."

"Nothing more for me," Lexie said. "But Renita will have a chardonnay."

Renita's hand shot up, palm out. "No, but thanks, anyway."

"I'll have a beer," Jack said.

"No, he won't," Lexie said to Brett as she rose to her feet. "Jack and I are leaving." She turned to her brother. "Remember you promised to help me with that cabinet door?"

"Yes, but *now?*" he said, frowning. "It's eleven o'clock at night."

"So? I work all night sometimes. This is early." Lexie took his arm and tugged him toward the door. "Bye."

"Let's catch up soon," Jack called back to Brett. "Sometime when I'm not doing handyman jobs on the night shift."

"I really do have to leave, too," Renita said.

"Stay," Brett said. "Just for one drink."

While she hesitated, he signaled the waiter and ordered wine for her and another beer for himself.

"So," he said, deciding not to tiptoe around the topic, "what was that all about, Lexie dragging Jack off?"

"That's just Lexie being weird," Renita said. "Don't pay any attention to her."

It had almost looked like matchmaking, if the idea of him and Renita together didn't seem so unlikely. Brett took a swig of beer. "You guys didn't look too happy tonight. Did something happen to Steve's dog?"

"He's alive, just," Renita said. "He ate fox bait set by the council in the creek reserve."

Brett winced. "That's bad." He'd seen a dog die after eating bait. It hadn't been pretty. "But he's alive, you say."

"We should know within the next twenty-four hours if he'll survive."

Brett sipped his beer. "It's not just the dog, is it?"

Renita twisted the stem of her wineglass, her mouth turned down. Finally, she cleared her throat. "My mother left my father."

"What—I understood she was at a retreat in Queensland."

Renita glanced away, blinking. "She rang him today to say she wanted to separate."

Steve and Hetty's marital problems were nothing to do with Brett, but his divorce was only six months old, recent enough for the pain to be fresh in his own mind. "That's a lot for Steve to handle on top of Smedley."

"He's so angry," Renita said, pleating a napkin. "He blames Hetty for Smedley nearly dying. Hetty thinks he loves his dog more than he loves her."

Brett scratched the back of his head. "How can Smedley eating fox bait be Hetty's fault?"

"All Dad ever wanted when he and Mother retired was for them to travel Australia in a trailer home. But my mother got into yoga." Now that Renita had started, she seemed to want to tell him the whole story. "She began changing, personal growth stuff, which is great for her but left Dad with too much time alone, especially when she went away on retreats. Then Dad got diabetes and now this happened with Smedley."

"It's rough." Brett wiped his thumb through the condensation on his glass. "But maybe if they're that different, they're better off apart."

"How can you say that?" Renita cried. "They can't give up on forty years of marriage just like that. They need to try to work it out."

"Some things can't be worked out," Brett replied. *Like your wife screwing your teammate in the bathroom at a party in your honor.* "Some things are too big to get over."

"Oh!" Renita seemed to pull herself up, as if recalling who she was talking to. "You're right. About some things."

No doubt she'd read about Amber's sexploits. Hell, the whole world knew. The unspoken subject brought an abrupt halt to their conversation.

Renita put down the napkin and fiddled with a cardboard coaster, rolling it through drops of water on the table. "Look, I'm sorry about the loan," she said, changing the subject. "I see a lot of small businesses start big and then fail within a year. It seemed to me you were biting off more than you could chew."

"Just because I got a few figures wrong the first time." He hated that he seemed stupid to her. He didn't know why her opinion should matter so much. The whole situation was all the more galling because his brothers had both done well in school and in business.

"It's not that I don't trust your business sense. But you admit you have no experience."

"No experience. Are you sure that's the only reason?" He suspected Renita, despite her denials, did hold a grudge, and he wanted to clear the air.

"What do you mean?" Her gaze raked his face.

He leaned forward, elbows on the table. "Back in high school I swear I didn't mean to hurt you—"

"You *didn't* hurt me." The words snapped out. "You couldn't hurt me."

"I was there, Renita. I saw your face." Even now her cheeks flamed red in the dim lighting. "You took me by surprise. I never thought of you—"

"That way?" she interjected coolly. "You never thought of me in a romantic light—is that what you're trying to say?"

He leaned back, shifting uncomfortably, and swigged his beer. Despite the air-conditioning the night was humid, and he was sweating. She was right, of course, but it didn't reflect well on him. So he said nothing.

"I was *embarrassed,*" Renita stressed, "because you and your friends were laughing at me. I wasn't *hurt*. Being hurt would imply I cared about what you thought of me. I didn't."

"So who did you end up going to the dance with?" he asked. After that day in front of the locker room he hadn't given her another thought. Now he wished he'd been kinder. God, he'd been a prick, really.

Renita stared at him. "Who did I go with?" She laughed. "This really hot guy in my English class. He bought me a corsage and picked me up in a limo.

We had champagne, stayed at the Grand Hyatt." She waved her wineglass. "It was like a fairy tale come true."

Jeez, he hoped she'd had a date. Somebody, *anybody*. "No, really, tell me."

She set her glass on the soggy coaster. "I sat at home the night of the prom and watched a movie with my parents. That was my sad, pathetic life. Are you happy now?"

Crap. Back then he'd liked Renita in a way he hadn't liked more popular girls. She'd known he struggled with his schoolwork, yet she'd always made him feel as if he could master it. If only he made the effort, which, admittedly, he rarely did.

"We were pals once, though," he said. "Weren't we?"

"Pals. Yeah, sure." She gave him a twisted half smile.

He realized suddenly what was different about her. "You're not wearing glasses."

"You just noticed." As if that confirmed something about him. And about her. "I got contact lenses."

He felt the way he did sometimes with Tegan, as if Renita had metamorphosed before his very eyes.

She rose and reached for her purse hanging on the back of her chair. "I've got to go. Thanks for the drink."

Brett got up, too, his thoughts jumbled. With any other friend he would have kissed her cheek.

While he stood there wondering how to say goodbye, she slipped out the door.

RENITA JOGGED ON THE SPOT in the small parking lot on Cliff Road where she'd arranged to meet Brett. She was dreading the coming ordeal. It all seemed so pointless anyway, after she'd stepped on the scales this morning and found she'd regained two pounds. After she'd been dieting and exercising like crazy for two weeks! To make herself feel better she'd eaten two bagels. With butter. And jam.

The other night in the pub had been mortifying. Of course Brett didn't think of her romantically. He never had. Never would. Pals. Friends. She *knew* that. She'd known it back in high school. It shouldn't hurt so much.

She started doing jumping jacks, her ponytail flopping over the shoulders of her baggy T-shirt. What she hadn't expected was how sensitive *he'd* been about his business acumen. His brothers had done well for themselves, one as a financial consultant, the other as an accountant. Maybe Brett felt like the dumb one in his family, just as she was a couch potato compared to Jack and Lexie. It was silly. Brett was a lot smarter than he gave himself credit for. He just didn't work at it. Or at least he hadn't in the past.

Brett jogged toward her around the bend in the road. He must have run here straight from home. In his sleeveless T-shirt and jogging shorts he looked like a freaking Greek god.

"Morning." He came to a halt with a spurt of gravel. "Feeling peppy?"

"Oh, yeah," Renita said, already breathless from her warm-up. "Peppy, that's me."

"Where's Steve? He was supposed to come, too."

"He's at home, nursing Smedley."

"Okay, here's the plan then," he said. "We'll alternate one minute running with two minutes walking. To the end of Cliff Road, down the path to the beach, double back along the sand and up the cliff at the other end, finishing back in this parking lot. That's three miles, about a third of the distance of the Fun Run."

"I can do that. Yep, no problem." She made fists and punched the air, trying to psych herself up.

He set off in the direction he'd come, jogging slowly. "How's Steve? He hasn't been back to the gym yet."

"I'm getting really worried," Renita admitted. "He doesn't leave the house. Just spends his time caring for his dog and brooding about Mum."

"I'll drop by and have a chat with him."

"I guess it couldn't hurt. He's not listening to us."

They ran in silence for a while, the steady thud of their running shoes on the pavement forming a rhythmic counterpoint to the cries of the gulls wheeling offshore.

"Is it a minute yet?" Renita puffed.

Brett consulted his stopwatch. "Nearly…. Okay, walk."

"Which one is your house?" Renita asked, slowing gratefully.

"That's my place on the next corner. The two-story terra-cotta one with the tiled roof."

Of course it was. The biggest, fanciest house in a block full of big fancy houses. "You must get a great view of the lights of Melbourne from that upper balcony."

"I bought close to the beach so Tegan could have easy access to the sailing club."

"I bet it's beautiful inside. I'll bet you have really nice chairs." She shot him a glance. "That wasn't a hint for you to invite me in to sit down or anything."

"Time to run. Hut, hut, hut…."

Renita groaned and broke into a jog.

"Keep up, Thatcher," he said, jogging backward ahead of her. "Get your ass in gear."

She took a swipe at him but he dodged the blow. "No fair, you're faster than I am."

"Train harder."

"Yeah, yeah," she grumbled. "Slave driver."

They came to the end of the road, a cul-de-sac with a lookout over the bay. Below, on the curving crescent of white sand, stood a row of colorful beach huts wedged among the bushes against the cliff, next to the sailing club. Kayaks and sailing dinghies dotted the beach above the high tide line.

Brett went first down the steep dirt path, then turned left, jogging away from the beach huts toward the rocky point where slabs of black basalt stretched into the water. Renita fell behind, bogged down in the soft sand.

She stopped at the rocks. Even alternating running and walking her lungs were burning. "Five minutes rest, that's all I ask."

Brett jogged back to her. "Okay, five minutes."

A bead of sweat dripped from her temple, tracked down her neck. She caught his gaze following the path between her breasts before he looked away. Yes, they were on the small side, nothing like Amber's.

She turned to face the bay. The water was choppy, a dark azure flecked with white. The brisk breeze cooled her face, ruffled Brett's sweat-dampened hair. He smelled like tangy salt mingled with soap, sweat and shampoo.

"About the other night—" Brett began.

"I think five minutes is up," she said, not wanting to revisit that conversation. "We should go."

He didn't move. In fact, he blocked her way when she would have gone around him. He held her arm just above the elbow, stopping her. "I lay awake last night, making up excuses for myself as a teenager."

"Forget it. It's in the past." She wished he would take his hand away. She couldn't think when he touched her.

"No, I have to say this." His eyes reflected the sky

and the sea, intensifying the blue of the irises. "There are no excuses. I was a jerk back then. I'm sorry."

Renita couldn't speak for the lump in her throat. She nodded, blinked. "I'm really not a pathetic loser holding a torch for a high school crush."

"I know that. You were intimidating in your own way."

"Who, me?" She laughed.

"You were so smart. You made me feel dumb." He tugged her ponytail the way he used to when they were teenagers. "Would you like to come to my place when we finish? I make a mean smoothie?"

A tendril of warmth curled through her despite her defenses and she smiled. "Sure. That sounds great."

Renita set off jogging again, slowly weaving her way through the rocks to the next sandy cove. Jogging and walking. Just her luck that they were back to jogging when the time came to climb back up the cliff. At this end of the beach the path wasn't as steep, but it was longer, doubling back on itself, the dirt studded with rocks and roots from the windswept ti trees growing out of the nearly vertical rock face.

Renita stumbled, her breathing labored. "You're doing great," Brett exclaimed. "Hang in there."

Nodding, she lurched around another bend in the path. With her jaw set, she spurted the last twenty meters to the top, staggered into the parking lot and bent forward, panting, her hands on her hips. "I did it."

"Congratulations. You've earned that smoothie."

Groaning, she straightened. Her legs felt wobbly. "We're driving to your house."

"Aw, come on, we can run. It's not far."

She fished in the inside pocket of her shorts for her car key. "It's miles to your place."

"One mile. You're such an exaggerator." Grinning, he added, "You drive, I'll run. I bet I can beat you."

"Shut up and get in the car." She hid a smile as she bent to unlock the door.

CHAPTER SEVEN

RENITA KICKED OFF HER sandy running shoes at the door and followed Brett into a two-story circular foyer. The sound of pop music drifted down from the second floor.

Next to the central curving staircase a fountain burbled out of tropical foliage into a koi pond where glints of gold flashed among the stones. Original artwork adorned the walls. Asian carved teak statues guarded the entrance. The decor was lavish and luxurious, a touch ostentatious.

She managed—just—not to let her jaw drop to her knees. Whatever Brett's financial problems, he hadn't trimmed his lifestyle. Renita gestured to the opulence around her. "How can you afford all this? Even if you're mortgaged to the max you must have had to put down a hefty deposit."

"Not that it's any of your business—"

"Of course it's my business. You sank all your cash into a fancy house and then came to the bank for more money. This is just like you. You want it all, and you want it now."

He stared at her, blinking, then said, "You knew

where I lived. Did you think I was eating off apple crates?"

Renita poked her head into the dining room. A crystal chandelier hung over a polished table that would seat twelve. "Why don't you borrow against the equity in the house? You didn't even include it as an asset in your loan application."

"I have hardly any equity, barely more than the minimum deposit. I don't want to take a chance on losing it. Tegan loves this place. She can walk to the beach and her sailing lessons in five minutes."

"You could drive her to her lessons from a cheaper area. Or she could ride a bike." Renita was back in the foyer, listening to the faint echo of her voice in the two-story atrium.

"Look, she's been through a rough time, with all the publicity surrounding my divorce," Brett said, following her. "Tegan had to leave the city and her school and all her friends."

"So this house is her consolation prize?"

"I want her to have the best. All the things that *I* didn't have growing up. Do you like mango? I bought some yesterday." The finality in his tone told her the conversation was over.

"Mango's great." Renita shook her head, unable to understand how a person could live so far beyond his means. She thought of her own small house, which she'd struggled to save for and was still paying off.

"Living room's through there," Brett said, pointing to the opposite side of the foyer from the dining room. "Have a seat. I'll just be a minute."

Renita walked through an arched doorway into a spacious room lined with plush carpeting and furnished with cream leather furniture and hand-crafted wooden tables. She sat on the buttery leather couch and gazed at the treasures strewn around. A bronze Remington bronco buster, a colorful blown glass vase dripping with gold leaf. It was like a museum.

"Most of my possessions I acquired over the years," Brett said, coming through the other doorway with tall glasses of the fruit concoction. "They mean something to me. Do you expect me to sell everything I own? Do I have to be destitute before the bank will give me a business loan?"

"I guess not." She sipped the smoothie he handed her.

Spying a silver-framed object on the marble mantelpiece, she rose and walked over to have a look. Just as she thought. It was his Brownlow Medal, a bronze shield twined with scrollwork and inscribed with the name Charles Brownlow, the original recipient, in 1924. The iconic words typed on white card beneath the medal read *Best and Fairest*. She had to admit the description was apt. Brett had been the most popular player for a decade and was still an influential figure in the Australian Football League. He'd given his time to charities and mentored young players, as well as being a sought-after and highly paid player.

"I remember watching the awards ceremony on TV the year you got this," she said.

Brett joined her by the fireplace. "I didn't know you were a footy fan."

"When you grow up with my dad, you watch a lot of sport." She traced a finger over the glass. "It must be hard to retire from a job you love."

"You don't go into professional sport thinking it will last forever. I got a few more years out of it than most. But, yeah, I miss playing." He took the medal from her, blew on the glass and polished it with the hem of his shirt. Then he put the Brownlow back on the mantelpiece, adjusting the frame so it sat a little taller.

Footsteps thudded on the stairs and Tegan appeared, wearing pink leggings under a purple skirt with a pink top. Her hair was pulled up in a messy bun and studded with sparkly clips. "Dad, can you take me shopping now?"

Judging from Brett's expression, Tegan's request had clearly come out of the blue. "Renita's here," he said. "Aren't you going to say hello?"

"Hey, Renita," she said. "Well?"

Renita moved over to a bookcase and pretended to peruse the titles, but couldn't help overhearing their conversation.

"I've got things to do this afternoon. You just went clothes shopping with your mother on the weekend."

"She had to cut it short for some lunch for the

Children's Hospital. I thought you and I could go to Chadstone Shopping Center."

"That's forty-five minutes away," Brett protested.

"Please, Dad," Tegan begged. "I really need a dress for the school dance. You never do anything with me."

Renita cleared her throat. "I should get going, anyway. You go, spend some time with your daughter."

"It's okay," Brett said. "I'll handle this."

She held up her hands. "I'm just saying."

He turned back to his daughter. "It's not just because Renita's here. I have to go to the gym shortly. The grand opening is coming up in a couple of weeks. I've got flyers to get printed, a program to develop. Plus I've got a class to teach this afternoon."

Tegan clamped her mouth shut and turned away. Renita became more uncomfortable. Poor kid. She'd just been through her parents' divorce, and now Brett was pouring all his time into his gym. If he wanted her to be happy, he should spend time with her instead of installing her in a big house.

"I could take her after I go home and shower and change," Renita offered, before she could think about what she was saying. "I was planning to do some shopping, anyway."

"That's very generous of you," Brett said. "I don't want to impose."

Tegan looked mutinous.

"It's no imposition. I don't mind going to Chadstone." Albeit not with a sullen teenager who made no secret of the fact that she resented any minute Renita spent with Brett. She hoped she didn't end up regretting feeling sorry for the girl.

"It's okay with me," Brett said. "Tegan?"

His daughter shrugged. "I guess so."

"You mean, 'Thank you, Renita, for being so kind.'"

"Thanks," Tegan muttered. "I'll go get changed." She ran back upstairs.

"This will be fun," Renita said brightly.

BRETT WRESTLED WITH HIS guilt over Tegan all the way to the gym. He vowed that as soon as everything was up and running smoothly he would spend more time with her. Maybe he would go out with her in the sailing dinghy one day.

He was grateful Renita was willing and able to relieve him of this girl stuff, but he wondered if she had any idea what she was getting into, the traipsing from store to store to store, with Tegan trying on a million outfits and rejecting them all.

A van was parked out front of the gym and workmen were carrying in rolls of carpet to be installed in the group fitness room. With fresh color on the walls and new flooring, the place was starting to feel like his. However, the improvements highlighted that the exercise equipment was old, broken or out-of-date.

Janet and Matt were in a huddle at reception, talking in low voices. When they saw him, they broke apart.

"Hey, guys," he said, dropping his gym bag in the cubbyhole of an office. "What's up?"

"Take a look." Janet pushed a flyer across the counter.

Coming Soon! Bayside Fitness Center...

Brett quickly perused the advertisement for a new gym opening next month on the outskirts of Summerside. It must be the construction site he'd noticed on the highway next to the hardware superstore. He'd thought his competition in Frankston and Mornington was bad enough. Now he had to contend with another gym right on his doorstep.

Photos showcased the architect's vision of the new facilities. Big red letters offered deals on memberships and extolled the numerous classes and services.

"They've got a swimming pool and sauna," Matt noted.

"It's too huge and impersonal," Janet scoffed. "We've got a friendly atmosphere and personal service."

What sparked the red haze in Brett's brain was the picture of rows and rows of brand-new exercise machines. Scowling, he crumpled the flyer and tossed it into the bin. "Who cares? Let's get to work."

Matt glanced toward the cluster of women in shorts and dance pants drifting through the front door. "I've got to teach a Zumba class."

"I'm doing the layout for the newsletter." Janet clicked the computer mouse and brought the screen to life. "I have twenty-five words to fit in about the new line of health drinks on sale. Do you think I can find space?"

"When you're done with that can you start designing a flyer for the grand opening?" Brett asked her.

"Sure thing, boss."

Brett headed for the inner office. He sat at the tiny desk wedged between filing cabinets and bookshelves filled with manuals on fitness. Grimly, he fired up his computer and did a search for used exercise equipment. In his opinion, buying secondhand was like throwing away money. But he couldn't delay any longer if he wanted a full complement of machines in time for the official opening.

Janet appeared in the doorway. "Should I put something in the newsletter about the opening—" She broke off as she noticed the website onscreen. "I thought you were going to buy new machines."

"I don't have the money." Just saying the words caused his chest to constrict with a physical pain that made him wince.

"But your loan?" she said, her expression stricken.

"It wasn't enough," he said bluntly. "And since I haven't won the lottery, and a truckload of thousand dollar bills hasn't fallen out of the sky…"

Janet swore under her breath. "What are you going to do?"

Brett *wanted* to punch a hole in the wall. Instead,

he nodded to the screen. "I'll buy a few used machines to replace the broken ones. It's not the end of the world."

It only felt like it.

It felt like all the times when he was a boy and his parents, unable to afford some essential item new, were forced to go to the Salvation Army store. Brett tried to tell himself there was no shame in buying secondhand; it was a more environmentally sound option.

But Renita was right; he wanted it all and he wanted it now. What was wrong with that, if he was willing to work hard for it? A man never got anywhere if he didn't think big and act bold.

He found the machines he needed, but his fingers hesitated over clicking on Buy Now. No matter how much he rationalized that there was no shame in buying secondhand, that it was temporary, a short-term solution to a problem he would eventually be able to fix, in his gut it still felt like failure.

Failure in his eyes, in his employees' eyes. In the eyes of his gym members.

Brett clicked out of the website without bookmarking the page. He would find the money on his own. He would show them all.

Brett O'Connor didn't fail.

"DON'T GET ME WRONG, I appreciate this," Tegan said as she walked through the brightly lit marble halls of Chadstone Shopping Center two paces ahead of

Renita. "Just don't think it's going to win you points with my father."

Renita caught up and passed Tegan, halting directly in front of the girl, forcing her to stop. "Let's get something straight. Number one, I am *not* interested in your father. Number two, you behave like a young lady and not a spoiled brat or I will get in my car and drive home. Without you."

"Dad wouldn't like that," Tegan warned. "He'd think you were irresponsible and mean."

Renita shrugged. "I don't care what he thinks of me." It wasn't true, but she refused to be held hostage by a snarky teenager. Without waiting to see if Tegan would agree to her terms, she walked off.

"Okay, okay." Tegan ran to catch up. "But you're going the wrong way. The teen stores are on the next level up. Don't you know anything?"

"That's it." Renita spun on her heel. "I presume you have enough money to take the bus home."

"No, wait," Tegan pleaded. "I'm sorry. Give me another chance."

"I warned you. You instantly tested me." How did parents put up with this all the time?

"If you stay I'll help you find a hot dress."

Unbelievable. Renita kept walking. "Why would I take fashion advice from someone less than half my age?"

"Because I know tons about style. My mum taught me everything there is to know about colors and silhouettes and fabrics." She gave a little skip. "*Every*thing."

Despite herself, Renita had to bite her lip to stop from smiling. The girl was irrepressible.

A shopfront caught her attention and she slowed. A cosmetic surgery clinic in the mall? She'd never seen that before. Posters advertised Botox injections, breast reduction and augmentation, liposuction….

Tegan stood next to her, studying the before and after photos. "Are you thinking of getting a boob job?"

Renita glanced sharply sideways. "Why do you ask that?"

Tegan's gaze flicked to Renita's breasts and back to the posters. "No reason."

"No, seriously, why?" Renita had always been self-conscious, less confident with men because of her small breasts. When she lost weight, the first place it went was from her breasts. Or so it seemed. Was her inadequacy obvious even to Tegan?

"If I say anything you'll get mad and drive off."

"Never mind, I don't want to know." Renita started to walk again.

Tegan followed. "My mum got hers done. Twice."

Renita didn't want to hear about Amber's big tits. Brett had divorced the woman for a reason, but she bet it wasn't because her breasts were too big.

She arrived at the escalator and turned to Tegan. "Okay, we'll shop. This is your last chance."

The teen stepped onto the rising staircase. "You won't be sorry. I promise."

Two hours and a dozen boutiques later, Tegan finally chose a multicolored wisp of silk with spaghetti straps and a handkerchief hemline.

Now it was Renita's turn. Trawling through shops with Tegan had given her respect for the girl's fashion savvy. She was every bit as knowledgeable as she'd claimed to be. Renita didn't *need* a new dress, except maybe for Jack and Sienna's wedding reception in a couple of months. But she'd lost the two pounds she'd regained, plus over the past four weeks another five, for a total weight loss of seven pounds. And all the exercise was starting to tone her muscles. She had "thin" dresses in her closet but they were several years out-of-date.

"What do you think?" Renita held up a lilac silk sheath against her body and turned to Tegan.

The girl, arms laden with dresses, shook her head. "Nope. Not party material."

"Why not?" Renita truly wanted to know. She wasn't good at fashion. Clothing had always been utilitarian—quality suits for work, T-shirts and jeans for leisure. That had been fine in the past. Now that she was losing weight and getting fit she wanted more. She wanted to shine.

"It's not sexy enough," Tegan explained. "You need either a low neckline or a low back. And the dress needs to cling. No offense, but that one would make you look like a tree trunk, straight up and down."

"I know I'm still on the heavy side."

"The point is, you've got curves. Show them off." Tegan started hanging the dresses inside Renita's fitting room.

"Your mother taught you well."

"Yeah." The hangers clacked busily as Tegan sorted the clothes.

"Do you see her much?"

"Every second weekend." Tegan picked out a couple of dresses, checking labels. "She's really busy most of the time. She's always got a party or some big do on. Charity work, so I'm not allowed to complain."

She peeled a red halter dress and a black cocktail gown from her bundle and handed them to Renita. "Try these on and then come out and show me."

"I never wear red—" Renita began.

"Shh!" Tegan held up a finger. "Never say never." She wagged the finger. "And don't decide in the cubicle that it's not you. I want to see."

"All right, Miss Bossy Boots."

Renita tried the black one on first. It was a simple cut with a low back and a slightly flared skirt that clung loosely to her hips. She piled her hair up on top of her head, then let it fall, noticing the ragged ends. It was time she had a trim.

Tegan was waiting outside the fitting room.

"I love this," Renita said, smoothing the fabric over her hips. "It feels fantastic."

"Hmm, it's too safe." Tegan's head tilted to one side, her blond ponytail swaying. "Try the red."

"Red isn't my color," Renita said, trying to explain again.

"You can wear any color as long as the shade is right." Tegan made shooing motions with her hands. "Hurry. We still have to shop for shoes."

Renita took off the black dress. She checked the label and did a double take. She'd dropped a whole dress size. Then she eased the red halter dress over her head. It was a snug fit and she had trouble getting it over her hips. Her bra showed above the low neckline.

"It's no good," she called over the top of the fitting room door. "Too small."

"Show me," the girl demanded.

Renita slunk out of the cubicle, arms crossed protectively over her chest. "See?"

Tegan circled her, tugging at the stretchy fabric. "It's not too small. It's supposed to be tight. Take your bra off."

"What? *No.* It's too revealing." And her boobs weren't big enough to fill out the bodice.

"Just do it." With her hands planted on her hips, Tegan reminded Renita of Brett when he was coercing her into another rep of sit-ups.

"Okay, okay." She went back inside, took off her bra and readjusted the dress.

Yikes.

That was a lot of bare skin. Turning, she looked

over her shoulder for the side and back view. She had to admit her exercise regime was paying off.

She thought about the string of gorgeous women who'd paraded through Brett's life—which she'd been privy to, courtesy of women's magazines and the society pages. They were all, especially Tegan's mother, glamorous to a fault.

Renita had never been glamorous in her life. Just once she would like to look as if she belonged on the red carpet.

"Renita?"

"Coming." She emerged a few minutes later with the gown over her arm. "I'm taking both dresses."

"Cool." Tegan gathered her shopping bags and Renita's, too. "Today wasn't as bad as I thought it was going to be."

"Gee, thanks," Renita said wryly. She studied Tegan's profile, the carefully lifted chin, the determined swing of the ponytail. "Are women really nice to you just to get to your dad?"

Tegan nodded. "As soon as they're actually expected to spend time with me, they suddenly have to go visit their sick grandmother or something."

"You're not so bad to hang with," Renita said. Tegan glanced at her, as if assessing her sincerity. Renita pretended not to notice. "How about a frozen yogurt before we head home? My treat."

Ultracasual, Tegan replied, "I guess that'd be okay."

THE MAROON DOOR WAS THREE steps below street level in a cobbled laneway. Brett walked past twice before he noticed the number tucked up high, beneath the ornate stone scrollwork. There was no sign, no advertisement and no hint of the nature of the business located here. Brett had gotten the name from the friend of a friend.

The door was locked. He rang the bell. And waited. A full twenty seconds passed before he heard soft footfalls and a key turning on the inside. The door opened.

A short bald man of about sixty, wearing a dapper suit with a blue silk tie, peered up at him through half-glasses perched on the end of his pointed nose. "Brett O'Connor."

"That's right. Mr. Toltz?"

"The same. Enter, please." Mr. Toltz turned and led the way across the narrow shop, between glass cases filled with shelves of coins, jewelry, war medals, old books, aboriginal artifacts and curiosities. Brett thought he glimpsed a Fabergé egg.

At the back of the shop was a large desk illuminated by a gooseneck lamp. It was littered with old coins and yellowing documents. Mr. Toltz gestured for Brett to sit as he cleared a space.

Then he lowered himself into his high leather chair and propped his hands over his rounded stomach. "Now, what do you have for me?"

Brett pulled the square leather box out of his

pocket. He opened the lid and set it on the desk in the pool of light.

Mr. Toltz took off his glasses, folded them carefully and laid them in an open case. He affixed a jeweler's loupe to his right eye. Brett fought the impulse to fidget as the older man studied the contents closely.

"Are you sure you want to part with this?"

Brett gripped his knees with white-knuckled hands, curbing the urge to grab the box and run. "How much can I get for it?"

"There's always a market for a Brownlow Medal. And when the owner is someone of your stature in the game, it'll be snapped up in no time." He turned it over and checked that Brett's name was engraved on the back.

"How much?" Brett repeated.

"The original Charles Brownlow Medal from 1924 sold recently for three hundred thousand. Len Thompson, also a popular Collingwood player, sold his for seventy-four thousand. But that was over ten years ago. You could expect more."

"How much more?"

"It's difficult to say."

"Ballpark."

"Somewhere between those two figures." Mr. Toltz shrugged his rounded shoulders. "One hundred and fifty thousand. Perhaps more."

Hopefully much more. "How soon could you sell it? And when could I expect to get the money?"

"Trouble with the loan sharks?" Mr. Toltz chuckled, his belly jiggling beneath his suit jacket.

Brett didn't crack a smile.

Mr. Toltz sobered. "A week or two. I'll put out a press release that an auction—"

Brett raised his hand. "No media." The last thing he wanted was a bunch of reporters digging into the circumstances surrounding the sale of his Brownlow. "I came here because I was told you're discreet. And because I can't wait for a public auction and all the advertising and publicity that goes with it. I need the money fast for a pet project of mine."

"All right," Mr. Toltz said. "I'll make inquiries among private collectors. I'm confident I can find a buyer within a few days."

Brett's shoulders sagged. Selling his medal was a form of taking action, which meant he was back in control. He would have the gym he wanted.

But at a cost he'd never thought to pay.

CHAPTER EIGHT

RENITA WAS SHOCKED at the state of Steve's house. Dirty clothes were strewn everywhere; empty beer cans and take-out wrappings cluttered the coffee table. "I'm leaving the front door open to air this place out. It stinks in here."

"Housework is Hetty's job," her dad grumbled. Wearing an undershirt and baggy cotton boxers, he sat on the couch, one hand resting on Smedley's back. The dog slept curled on a thick towel, his brown muzzle tucked between his paws. On newspaper spread over the floor were bowls of kibble and water.

"She can't do it if she's not here, can she?" Renita demanded, stacking dishes onto a tray with a clatter. "Why should it be *her* job? You're both retired. What else do you have to do? Jack said you've even stopped going to the Men's Shed."

"I have to take care of Smedley."

"He's going to be all right. The vet said so."

Renita was relieved that Steve hadn't gone back to eating the cakes and cookies that aggravated his type 2 diabetes. He'd learned something, at least. But a steady diet of take-out food was almost as unhealthy for him.

A brisk knock was followed by Brett's voice calling through the open door, "Hello! Can I come in?"

Renita picked up the tray piled with dirty dishes and carried them out of the living room through the foyer. She blew back a wisp of hair that had escaped her ponytail. "What are you doing here?"

"Stopping in to see how Steve is doing."

"He's sulking." She gestured behind her with her head, then headed for the kitchen. "Go see for yourself."

Brett peered around the dividing wall into the living room, then joined her. "Is your father having a breakdown?"

"He's completely gone off the rails," she said, running hot water in the sink. "He was starting to see results with his exercise and diet, and now this. I've begged and pleaded. Nothing I say seems to penetrate. He's given up."

"Begging and pleading won't get you anywhere," Brett said. "I'll see what I can do."

"Go easy," she warned. "He's had a couple of bad shocks—first Smedley, then Mum."

"Did going easy work?"

"No, but—"

"He needs tough love. Trust me on this." Brett retraced his steps to the living room and stood in front of the couch, hands on his hips. "Yo, Steve!"

Steve opened his eyes and blinked. "Brett."

Renita stood at the archway, arms crossed, chewing on her thumbnail.

"I see your dog survived," Brett went on. "That's great."

Steve combed a hand across his disheveled gray hair, only messing it up more. "He was lucky."

"You've missed three personal training sessions. We need to reschedule you."

"I don't know…."

Brett scooped a stack of magazines off the armchair and dumped them on the floor. Sitting, he leaned forward, elbows on his knees. "Renita told me about Hetty. I guess you're angry."

Steve shrugged and glanced away.

"You *should* be angry," Brett said.

"I don't think—" Renita began.

He held up a hand to shush her. "Your wife can't just up and leave without warning, without making sure you're all right. That your dog is okay."

A faint spark glimmered in Steve's eyes. "That's right."

"Let me give you some advice from one who's been there," Brett said. "Don't let her make your life worse than it has to be."

"What do you mean?" Steve said. "How can it get worse?"

"If you don't take care of yourself, if you get sick again, that'd be worse, wouldn't it?"

"Sure, but…" Steve blinked, nonplussed.

"You need to reinvent yourself, the sooner the better. Get yourself in shape. If you feel good, look good, and are doing great things, she's going to be sorry she left you. She's going to feel like a fool."

Oh, man, Brett was talking revenge, exactly the same as she'd planned for him. It didn't sound very nice, hearing it spelled out so coldly. Calculatingly.

"Excuse me, Brett," Renita said. "I don't think this is the way to—"

"Shh. Let me do this."

Steve pushed his fingers across his comb-over and sat up straighter. "Do you think?"

"I *know*," Brett said. "Success is the best revenge. Women aren't interested in losers who sit around in their underwear, drink beer and get fat and pasty-faced. They want a winner."

"I don't know," Steve said, shaking his head.

"You can be a winner," Brett insisted. "But you've got to get off your butt. Get back to the gym. Throw out the crap food and learn to cook."

"Cooking's women's work," Steve scoffed.

"Not at all. The best chefs in the world are men."

"Oh, please." Renita rolled her eyes.

Brett continued to ignore her. "Your son, Jack, cooks. Women really go for a guy who knows his way around the kitchen. You want romance, learn to make risotto. Women will be beating a path to your door."

"I'm too old to be looking for someone new," Steve said, slumping back down.

"Exactly." Renita walked into the room and stood between the two men, facing Brett. "Listen, you. He wants my *mother* back. That's what we should be working on."

Brett stood and moved her aside, speaking directly to Steve. "You're never too old for romance. It's either that or you lie down and die right now. Is that what you want?"

"No, I don't," Steve said. "Smedley would miss me."

"*I* would miss you." Renita turned to him, exasperated. "We all would. *Especially Mother.*"

"So what are you going to do?" Brett asked Steve.

"I'll think about what you said."

"That's a start," Brett stated. "You could take a cooking class. Or get Jack to teach you. I could show you a few recipes. My seared scallops and chorizo is a big hit with the babes."

"*Babes?*" Renita choked out. "Dad needs to convince Mum to go to couples counseling, not start over as a gigolo."

Brett turned to her. Lowering his voice, he asked, "Do you want your father to be happy?"

"He'll be happy if my mother comes back."

Brett took her arm and led her away a few paces. "But would she be happy with him the way he is now? Isn't this partly why she left?"

"It's not that simple," Renita said.

"Of course it isn't. But you pleading with him to

take care of himself isn't going to make a blind bit of difference. He has to want to change for his own sake. I've given him a reason."

"But telling him to go out with other women—"

"Did I?" Brett's blue eyes gleamed. "Practically everything I said could be taken as ways for him to get your mother back." While Renita thought about that, he added, "Steve needed a prod. I gave it to him."

Her mouth tightened. She couldn't dispute that, but the way he did things was just so infuriating. If he got results…

If he got results she'd be happy, period. "Thanks for taking a personal interest in him. You didn't have to do that."

"All part of the service." Brett went back to her dad. "I want to see you at the gym tomorrow, bright and early."

Steve hesitated. "I'll try."

Mission accomplished, Brett walked to the front door and down the steps.

Renita followed and stood in the doorway. "Is that why you want your gym to be a success? So that Amber will be sorry and come back to you?"

Brett stabbed a finger in her direction. "The reason I want the gym to be a success is because I don't do anything half-assed."

"Oh, like the way you're such a wholehearted, attentive father?"

Brett recoiled as if she'd slapped him.

Renita put a hand over her mouth. It had just slipped out....

But Renita wasn't sorry. She'd been thinking it for a while.

"I appreciate you taking Tegan shopping, but don't..." He held up a hand in warning. "Don't you go there."

Then he got into his car and drove away.

LYNN SWIRLED the black hairdressing cape around Renita and fastened it at the neck. Blonde, blue-eyed and still pretty at nearly sixty years old, she reached for her comb and scissors. "The usual?"

Renita's heart beat rapidly. She'd worn her hair in the same style for years. Now she was starting to lose weight, she'd replaced her glasses with contact lenses, she had a sexy new dress. She didn't do things half-assed, either. She was making herself over.

"I want something different."

"Different?" Lynn smiled. "What kind of style?"

"Modern. Trendy. Edgy. Surprise me." *Gulp.* "I mean, as long as I don't end up looking like Ziggy Stardust or Amy Winehouse."

Lynn ran her fingers through Renita's thick wavy bob. "You've got great hair. I know just the haircut for you."

Renita gripped the arms of her chair. "Let's do it."

"Color, too?" Lynn asked. "Do you want to go blonde?"

"No." She wanted to be herself, only…better. "But you could put in some highlights. Or lowlights. Whatever they're called. Do you have time to do all this?"

"I'll fit you in, don't worry. This is so exciting." Lynn bustled away to mix the color.

While she waited, Renita picked up a women's magazine and idly flipped through the pages. Naturally there was a photo of Amber at a red carpet event. She certainly was high maintenance, with nails like talons, tattoos, spray-on tan, makeup worthy of a movie star. Amber had long blond hair à la Pamela Anderson. She bore another similarity to Pammy— huge breasts.

Renita glanced in the mirror and her mood dimmed a little. She'd been congratulating herself on her improved appearance, but she couldn't begin to compete with women like Amber. No matter how much weight she lost she'd still be a small-busted brunette.

With highlights, she consoled herself.

Anyway, it shouldn't matter what she looked like. Personality, intelligence, kindness and character were what counted.

Sure they were. That's why Amber, ex-manicurist, party girl and cheater, was standing on a red carpet surrounded by celebrities. While Renita, quiet living and loyal, could only dream about having a man like Brett.

The thought brought her up short. She was over Brett.

She was a grown woman, no longer susceptible to teenage fantasies. Being older and more experienced, she could see Brett's faults as clearly as she could ogle his good looks. His neglect of Tegan made her as angry as his charm made her weak in the knees. His impatience to refurbish the gym frustrated her as thoroughly as his concern for her father warmed her.

Her worried eyes stared back at her from the mirror.

Lynn returned, stirring a plastic cup of hair coloring. She sectioned Renita's hair with a comb and teased out a few strands over a piece of aluminum foil. With a brush she began painting on the color. "You've lost weight, haven't you? Have you met someone?"

Renita denied it. But by the time Lynn had colored, cut and blown Renita's hair dry, she'd heard all about her personal training sessions with Brett, Smedley's poisoning and an abridged version of Hetty and Steve's problems. In turn Lynn updated Renita on the doings of her grandchildren and the on-again, off-again relationship with her Russian boyfriend. She'd also updated her on Amber's split with her other footy player.

Three hours later Renita left the salon, feeling like a new woman. She floated down the street, glancing into shop windows to check out her reflection. The chin-length cut was layered and bouncy, with dark gold highlights that brought out the natural hint of red in her dark brown hair and gave her a warm glow that matched the way she felt inside.

She was too keyed up to go home, so she drove over to Lexie's house to show off her new do. Sienna's car was parked out front. Even better.

She rang the doorbell and just walked in as usual. Hearing the TV, she veered left toward the living room. "Lexie?"

Oliver was sitting on the rose-patterned chintz couch in his school uniform, gray pants and green polo shirt. Yin, Lexie's cream-colored Burmese cat, lay curled on his lap. Yang, the chocolate Burmese, was stretched out behind Oliver's head on the back of the couch. The boy glanced away from an old episode of *Get Smart* and did a double take. "Renita?"

"Hey, Olly," Renita said, grinning. "Yep, it's me."

"You look so different."

"I just had my hair done. Do you like it?"

"Sure, I guess." He motioned with his head toward the backyard. "Mum and Lexie are out in the studio."

"I'll find them." Renita started to go through the door then paused. "By the way, do you know Tegan O'Connor? I think she's in your class at school."

Oliver's nose wrinkled. "The new girl? It's cool that her dad's a famous footy player, but she's kind of stuck-up."

Renita could see how Tegan could come across that way. "It's hard to break into a new school where everyone already knows each other."

Oliver stroked Yin. "How do you know her?"

"Her father owns the gym I go to." She paused. "Are you going to the dance?"

"Prob'ly."

"Could you talk to her? Maybe ask her for a dance?"

He groaned. "Do I have to?"

"It would be a nice gesture. Think about it."

Renita walked through the house and across the backyard to the detached studio, where Lexie was working on a portrait of Sienna. Renita approached the open door cautiously. Her sister didn't like to be disturbed when she was painting. But for Renita to get a new hairstyle was as novel as an alien invasion in Summerside.

The third version—or possibly a fourth—of Sienna's portrait was on the easel. One of the paintings would be entered into the competition for the Archibald Prize, a prestigious nation-wide contest. Renita thought they *all* looked amazing.

She waited out of sight while Lexie finished painstakingly stroking in what appeared to be every single hair on Sienna's pre-Raphaelite head. Lexie and Sienna were talking about babies. Both women were in their late thirties. Sienna wanted to get pregnant. She had a good chance, now that she and Jack had found each other. But Lexie was single. Renita felt a tug at her heart, hearing the yearning in her sister's voice even as she denied that she wanted a baby.

At a natural pause in the conversation, Sienna happened to glance up. "Oh, my God!" she squealed. "Renita, you look fantastic!"

Lexie's brush jogged and she turned. Seeing her, she gasped. "Wow. Just, *wow!*"

"Sorry to interrupt. I had to show someone." Renita fluffed her layers and twirled. "You like?"

Lexie pressed paint-stained fingers to her cheeks. She still held her paintbrush, and now a streak of burnt umber wove through her long blond waves. "I *love*. You look gorgeous."

"Pretty soon we won't recognize you," Sienna said.

Renita basked in their admiration. "Come on," she said in a token protest. "It's just me. I'm still the same person."

But even as she said it, she wondered if it was true.

THE CALL CAME IN the evening. Dinner was over and Tegan was upstairs, doing homework. Brett was tidying up the kitchen and checked his caller ID. His heart rate kicked up. "Hello, Mr. Toltz. Any news?"

"There's been a great deal of interest. As per your instructions, my inquiries were conducted with the utmost secrecy," Simon Toltz said in his precise, pedantic way.

"Does any of that interest translate into someone actually wanting to hand over money?"

"Oh, yes." The agent practically chortled. "This afternoon I presided over a brief but intense bidding war."

Brett paced the room. "And…?"

"The final bid, which I accepted on your behalf, also per your instructions to balance a speedy sale with maximum price, was $190,000."

"Say that again?" Brett's heart was beating so loudly he could hardly hear.

"One hundred and ninety thousand dollars."

Brett dropped onto a kitchen chair with a thump. He released a noisy breath. "How long before I can get the money?"

"I should have a bank check couriered to you by the end of the week."

"Thank you very much, Mr. Toltz. It's been great doing business with you." Brett discussed details of the transaction with the dealer and then hung up.

His mind whirled. He still had thirty-odd thousand left of the second loan. That would be enough to put down a deposit on new exercise equipment. Once the check for the Brownlow Medal was cleared into his bank account, he could pay the balance.

He had the fizzing-with-excitement, slightly sick feeling he got when running out onto the field before a big game. The roaring in his ears seemed to come from a faraway crowd, cheering him on.

Action. It's what he'd trained so hard for all his life. It's what he was good at.

He ran upstairs to his bedroom and from the top of his dresser took down his manila folder with the itemized list of exercise machines. Seating himself at the desk, he booted up his laptop. His body hummed along with the computer.

The website he wanted was bookmarked. A few keystrokes sent him to the order form. He started checking boxes, six of this, six of that. He had to do without a couple of items because he didn't have quite enough money. But close enough. Bloody well close enough.

He filled in his bank account details, authorizing a direct debit for the deposit on Monday of the following week. He held his finger poised over the submit button, savoring the triumph of the moment.

Then, taking a deep breath, he hit Send.

After that, Brett was so pumped that even though it was nearly dark he put on his shorts and running shoes. He needed to get rid of some of his energy.

"Tegan," he called over her pop music as he passed her bedroom. "I'm going for a run."

Her door burst open. "First can you sign this form saying you're going to chaperone the dance? I have to take it back to school on Monday."

"Oh, right." The dance. He wasn't looking forward to spending the evening riding herd on a bunch of teenagers. "Why do you want me to do this so badly? Most kids wouldn't want their parents at a dance," he said, reading over the information.

"If you go, then I'll know at least *someone* will talk to me."

He glanced up in surprise. Where had his confident-to-the-point-of-cocky daughter gone? "Don't the other kids talk to you?"

"They're all stuck-up."

"What about Amy?"

Tegan shrugged, her mouth turned down, a crease between her eyebrows. "She didn't choose me as a partner for sailing. The instructor put us together."

Brett's conscience pricked. Tegan was unhappy. And he knew practically nothing about what was happening in her life. How would he? He spent all his time at the gym. And when she spoke to him he barely listened. Remorse dampened the exhilaration of his purchases.

"You're going to be the prettiest girl there," he told her as he scribbled his name. "You can be my date."

Tegan took the form and gave him a hug, "Thanks, Daddy."

She hadn't called him Daddy in years. He hugged her back extra hard. "I'll be home soon, kiddo. Then we'll watch a movie together."

He headed down the stairs, pausing in the foyer to glance through the arched doorway at the fireplace. And the empty spot on the mantelpiece. Selling his

Brownlow Medal had been like selling a piece of himself.

He should have told Tegan. She'd been with him and Amber at the awards night when he'd won the medal. His daughter was the most important person in his life. How had he let himself get so estranged from her?

He knelt to tie his running shoes with jerking motions. The medal was gone. He had to get used to it. In its place he would have a bright, shiny Brett O'Connor Fitness Center.

Instead of taking his usual route he jogged in the other direction, away from the beach, up the hill. To Renita's. Okay, so he was gloating. He deserved to crow after she'd turned him down for the money, twice.

As he reached her driveway and approached the gray weatherboard house with white trim, an attractive woman with chin-length hair, wearing a softly clinging dress, came out of the house. It took him a moment to realize it was Renita. He stopped in his tracks.

She swung her purse over her shoulder, car keys jingling in her hand. "Hey, Brett."

"Renita." She looked so good he was hard-pressed not to whistle. "I like your hair."

"Thanks." She smiled.

"In fact, you're looking pretty hot."

She started to touch her hair, then caught herself. She nodded. "What's up?"

"I came to tell you I finally ordered gym equipment."

"Wonderful. What did you buy?"

"Treadmills, steppers, stationary bikes. I got everything I wanted." Just saying that made his spirits soar.

Renita came a step closer. "You must have got a good deal. I guess used equipment is a lot cheaper."

"I bought brand-new."

"But..." She frowned. "Where did you get the money?"

"I sold my Brownlow Medal." He said it sharp and hard, knowing she'd be shocked. Hell, he hoped she'd feel guilty.

"Your Brownlow? Oh, Brett!" Renita stared at him, as shocked as he'd hoped she would be. "You didn't."

"I had to."

"Is the gym worth that much to you?"

"*More*. I'm not going to be some has-been athlete reduced to coaching boys' football. Maybe in ten or fifteen years I'd like that. But right now, I want to build a business, make it grow and thrive."

"But your Brownlow!"

"I know." In truth, he felt as ill about that as she looked. But he had the equipment.

"How much did you get for it?"

"One hundred and ninety thousand dollars. That plus what I had left from the second loan was just enough to buy what I needed."

"This is awful. I—I don't know what to say."

"How about 'I'm sorry, Brett. I made a mistake in not trusting you.'"

Her expression turned cool. "I'm sorry you had to sell something so precious to you. I hope it was worth the sacrifice."

"Given the lack of support from my local bank, I didn't have any choice."

"No choice?" she repeated. "You had choices—to buy used, go slow, build slowly." She shook her head. "On second thought, we're talking about the most impatient man I know. Maybe you didn't have a choice. Was Tegan okay with selling the medal?"

Suddenly he lost the urge to rub Renita's nose in his success.

"Tegan understands." At least, he hoped she would one day.

"I hope so." Renita glanced down at her keys, picking out the one for her car. "You'll have to excuse me. I'm late."

It occurred to him suddenly that she might have a boyfriend. "Are you going on a date?" He'd just assumed she was single. A foolish assumption, he realized now.

"I'm going to J—" She broke off, lifted her chin. "I'm going out for dinner. Was there anything else?"

She looked so pretty. "Is that a new dress?" he asked.

"I've had it for a few years. I haven't been able

to fit into it until recently." She put the key in the car door.

His next words were out before he knew what he was saying. "This dance of Tegan's, the one I have to chaperone…"

Renita glanced up. "Yes?"

"I was wondering if you wanted to go with me." He hadn't planned to ask her. This encounter wasn't turning out at all the way he'd envisioned.

She stared at him. "You're asking me to the school dance?"

It seemed ludicrous when she put it that way. "I know it's not the most thrilling night out."

"I wouldn't know," Renita said drily. "I never went to a school dance."

Now who was applying the guilt?

"It won't be that much fun. Having your toes stepped on by clumsy boys, stopping kids from spiking the punch, and monitoring dark hallways for drunken, groping teenagers."

"You're really making this sound like an attractive proposition." She tilted her head to one side, setting a dangling earring swinging. "I just don't understand why you're asking me."

He was starting to wish he hadn't started this. Perspiration prickled around his hairline.

"Is it because Tegan wants you to have a date?"

"No." In fact, he realized belatedly, Tegan might not be happy about sharing him.

"Are you feeling sorry for me, or guilty over what

happened in grade eleven?" Renita asked sharply. "Because we've been over this. You don't need to, not for a second."

"No, it's not that, either."

"Then why?" She hesitated, as if the next question was a difficult one to ask. "Is it because of how I look now?"

Well, yeah. Until tonight it had never occurred to him to ask Renita out on a date. She'd changed. She'd become more desirable. Not just because of the weight loss, but her hair, contact lenses, new clothes…. What was wrong with him responding to that? Although even he was smart enough to understand she wouldn't see it the way a guy did.

"It would be more fun if you came with me," he said finally. "Do you want to go or not?"

"I'll check my diary to see if I'm available. Then I'll have to think about it. A high school dance is exciting when you're fifteen, but at thirty-two? As a chaperone?" She rolled her eyes. "Not so much."

Was she going for payback? She was sure as hell making him sweat. "It's next Saturday. Eight o'clock."

She unlocked her car and climbed in, leaving him with a glimpse of smooth bare calf. Then the driver's-side window rolled down. She smiled as she backed out past him. "I'll let you know."

CHAPTER NINE

RENITA PICKED THE OLIVES out of her salad and set them aside. Four of them equaled one Weight Watchers' point, the same as a small glass of wine. Wine versus olives? Wine won, hands down. Even so she would stretch a single glass out as long as possible. With Brett interested, she wasn't going to blow her diet now.

Jack's dining table buzzed with talk and laughter. The guests included Lexie and her date, Bruce, and Carl, a pilot friend of Jack's. Their dad had dragged himself away from Smedley's sickbed for the evening.

Renita leaned close to Lexie, who was sitting next to her. "Brett asked me on a date."

"Ooh!" her sister squealed.

"Shh!" Renita poked her in the ribs. "I haven't made up my mind yet."

"You did it! You've succeeded in capturing Brett's attention—after all these years."

"And now that I have it, I can see how immature I was being. I need to move on."

"But you've got him hooked. That's so cool."

"At first when he dropped by he was trying to make me feel bad because he sold his Brownlow Medal to pay for fitness equipment after I wouldn't lend him the money."

"Those medals mean a lot, don't they? I don't follow football, but even I know that."

"Yes, and I do feel bad. I feel sick about it."

"You had good reasons for not giving him the loan, though, right?"

"Bank guidelines are very strict. He seems to take it so personally, though. He was still angry."

"So why would he want to go out with you?"

"He wouldn't admit it, but I think it's because I look more attractive. Are men really that shallow? What about my personality? That hasn't changed."

"Maybe he always liked you. Now he desires you, too. Men are very visual. I don't see a problem." Lexie leaned forward eagerly. "Where is he taking you?"

"To help chaperone Tegan's school dance."

"Oh." She sat back.

"I know. It's not exactly a night on the town." Renita sipped her wine, savoring the taste all the more because she allowed herself so little.

"Do you want to go?" Lexie asked.

"It's an excuse to wear my new dress."

"Not a good enough reason." Her sister tucked her hair back with paint-stained fingers. "Do you like him?"

"He drives me crazy." She nibbled at a small

forkful of risotto, mentally counting calories. Jack didn't stint on butter and Parmesan.

"That doesn't answer my question." Lexie tipped her head to one side. "Or does it?"

"I don't know." Renita waved her fork. "I can't tell if what I'm feeling is a maudlin crush from high school or if I like the man he is now."

"*I* think he's terrific. You know the broccoli salad Dad brought tonight? Brett taught him how to make it."

Renita's eyebrows rose. "I thought Sienna made the salad."

"Nope. Dad was telling me about it before you arrived. Brett came over to his place earlier this week with all the ingredients. He made Dad watch and write down the recipe. That's over and above, in my opinion."

"And Dad actually followed up by making the dish," Renita mused. "He's starting to take responsibility."

Across the table, Jack began to tell an anecdote about the marathon he and Carl had recently competed in.

"We were neck and neck, with fifty yards to the finish line, when the guy beside Carl stumbled and fell," Jack said, holding the attention of the whole table. "Carl stopped to help him up and get him to the sidelines."

Carl waved off the general murmur of approbation. "Jack was pulling ahead. I took the easy out."

"Bull. You were a nose in front," Jack replied with a grin. "Tripping the competition was my only hope."

Amid the laughter, Lexie nudged Renita. "Carl's hot, isn't he? He's been glancing your way all evening."

"No way," Renita said automatically. Carl was an Iron Man athlete. Plus he was tall and good-looking. Men of his caliber didn't give her the eye.

"What about the guy you brought tonight—Bruce?" she asked her sister. "Is he 'the one'?"

With a rueful smile, Lexie shook her head. "He just broke up with his boyfriend. There are no good straight men my age who are single."

"Thirty-eight isn't old. You'll meet someone," Renita declared. "When you least expect it."

"I don't have time for a man right now, anyway," Lexie said. "I'm busy with my painting and will be for months." She pushed her empty plate away. "So, what are you going to do about Brett?"

Renita didn't answer immediately. Her feelings were so mixed up. That he'd gone back to give Steve a cooking lesson surprised her. Brett wasn't all talk. He cared about people.

So should she go to the dance with him, when she'd only considered it as a way of showing him what he was missing? That wasn't any better reason than wearing a new dress.

Tegan wouldn't like it, either.

"We'll have dessert in the living room," Sienna announced, rising. "Who wants coffee?"

As the group moved slowly into the other room, topping up wineglasses or getting water, Renita found herself next to Carl.

"I haven't had a chance to talk to you tonight," he said. "Jack told me he had sisters, but he didn't mention how attractive they were."

Renita felt the heat climb her cheeks. "Lexie's the pretty one."

"I don't know about that," Carl said, smiling. "I prefer brunettes."

He sat next to her on the couch, his thigh touching hers, his shoulders twisted slightly sideways so he could talk to her more easily. While they ate cheesecake—another thousand calories—he told her about his job as second officer on the jumbo jets that flew the Asia routes, and about his dog, a boxer named Mojo.

The evening gradually wound to a close. Steve left first, then Lexie and Bruce. Renita and Carl were left alone on the couch while Jack and Sienna carried cups and plates to the kitchen.

"It's getting late," Renita said, suddenly feeling self-conscious to be sitting so close.

"I'm flying to Bangkok tomorrow morning," Carl said. "Can I call you when I get back in a few days? I've got a small plane out at the airfield where Jack keeps his. We could fly up to Sydney for the day next weekend. Have lunch on the waterfront. What do you say?"

Renita blinked up at his ruggedly handsome face. He was interesting, well traveled, and he loved dogs. She ought to be jumping at the opportunity to get to know him better.

"I can't believe I'm going to turn down lunch in Sydney," she replied. "Next Saturday I have a date to go to my first high school dance."

BRETT WADED WAIST DEEP into the bay, pushing the twelve-foot fiberglass sailing dinghy out from shore. Tegan raised the sail and cleated it off. Then he levered himself aboard while she sat in the cockpit, one hand guiding the tiller.

She turned the small vessel broadside to the wind, heading out into the bay so they could go around the point. Behind them, receding in the distance, the row of colored beach huts nestled against the cliff. On the deck of the sailing club, members were enjoying Sunday brunch.

The morning had dawned clear with a light breeze clipping the foam off the waves. Brett had coaxed Tegan out of bed with blueberry pancakes, and enticed her down to the beach with the promise of a few hours on the water, just the two of them.

His daughter pushed windblown hair out of her face as she glanced up. "How come you're being so nice all of a sudden?"

"I don't know what you're talking about," Brett

said, keeping an eye out for shallow rocks. Water dripped off his board shorts into the cockpit, but his legs were already feeling the warmth of the sun.

"Videos last night, pancakes this morning." Tegan leaned forward and adjusted the sheet.

Brett repositioned his baseball cap before turning his attention to her. "There *is* something I want to talk to you about."

Tegan sat up straighter. "We're moving back to the city?"

"No," Brett said, surprised by the suggestion. "Why would you want to leave all this for the smog and traffic there?"

"Mum. My friends." Tegan glanced wistfully at the skyline of Melbourne in the distance. "Never mind. What did you want to talk about?"

Brett figured he'd better start with the smallest problem. Trouble was, he didn't know which that was—Renita or the Brownlow. "For one thing, I asked Renita to go to your dance with me."

Tegan's face fell. "You said *I* was your date."

When they went to the mall, Tegan walked five paces in front of him so no one would know she was out in public with her father. "Renita hasn't said yes," he replied. "She may not be able to come."

"But I thought you two were just friends."

"We *are* just friends." He'd asked her out on a whim; that didn't mean anything had changed between them. "Don't worry so much. At the dance you're going to be hanging with the other kids."

"They all hate me."

"Of course they don't hate you."

"You don't know what it's like."

"If it's that bad, then maybe we shouldn't go."

"I *have* to go."

"Why?"

Tegan didn't reply, for as they came out of the shelter of the point, a gust of wind pushed the boat ahead. She let out the sail, altering their course away from the rocks, and gripped the tiller hard, trying to hold it steady against the wind and current.

"Do you want me to steer?" Brett said, eyeing the waves surging over the black basalt boulders only yards away.

"I'm okay," she said, again scraping windblown strands of hair out of her eyes.

Brett kept his gaze on the rocks. "The other thing is I sold my Brownlow Medal."

Tegan glanced at him, wide-eyed. "You *what?*"

"I sold—"

"Never mind. I heard. How could you do that?"

"I didn't think you would care that much," he said, honestly surprised at the strength of her reaction.

"I remember the night you won that medal. You were so happy." Tegan blinked from the salt spray coming off the hull. "Whenever the sports guys talk about you on TV it's always Brett O'Connor, Brownlow Medal winner. How can you throw away something that means so much to you?"

"I didn't 'throw it away.'" Brett swiveled to meet

her teary blue eyes. "I needed the money to buy new exercise machines for the gym."

"The gym." Tegan's voice was flat with disbelief. "Everything's about the gym. Even this morning you only wanted to go sailing so you could tell me about the medal. Which is really about the gym, right?"

He'd been afraid she would take it this way. "The fitness center is my livelihood. I didn't want to sell my medal. I *had* to. I know the past few months have been tough. I haven't had much time for you. That will change, I prom—"

He broke off abruptly as, without warning, the sail ripped away from the sheet cleating it to the deck. The white triangle flapped wildly and the dinghy tilted, pushed across the bay by the wind, but without enough speed for the tiller to have any effect.

They were heading toward the rocks.

"Dad!" Tegan cried, her face white. "Do something!"

Brett grabbed a paddle and scrambled to the bow.

The dinghy hit a rocky outcropping and lurched, nearly throwing him out. Clinging to the mast with one hand, he used the paddle to push them off the rocks. With a loud scraping sound the small vessel slid sideways through the foaming waves. Tegan stood in the cockpit and grappled with the sail. She looped the sheet through the grommet and tied it off, then hauled the canvas in close. Brett paddled to bring the dinghy around.

Tegan huddled in the cockpit, the tiller tucked tightly to her side, still pale.

They were out of danger, heading for calmer water.

Brett stowed the paddle and went to sit next to her, wrapping an arm around her shoulders. "Are you all right?"

"I want to go back."

"We were lucky. It could have been worse." He rubbed her arm. "What happened there?"

"The knot holding the sail came loose."

A knot she'd tied.

"You did well, getting the dinghy back under control," he murmured.

She shrugged, huddled into herself.

"Don't worry. You'll practice your knots and get them right next time."

"I don't care about the knots or the stupid sailboat!" She brushed a hand across her eyes. "I told Oliver you'd show him your Brownlow Medal. It was the only thing I could think of to get his attention. Now you've sold it. Do you have any idea how embarrassing it's going to be to tell him?"

"Who's Oliver?" Brett asked.

"A boy at school. Renita knows him. They're related somehow."

Hell. Brett rubbed a hand over his face. "Oh, so you were worried about me losing the medal because it means so much to me, were you?"

"That's still true," she stated sullenly.

"Don't tell him," he said, exasperated. "Say it's locked away in a safety deposit box or something."

"He'll hear about the sale. It's going to be in all the newspapers. How could you do it, Dad?" she wailed. "No one sells their Brownlow Medal. No one but *losers*."

Brett tensed, but he kept his temper, determined not to react. "You don't need to use my medal to attract a boy. Just smile and be friendly. You're so lovely, Tegan. Just be yourself."

"Myself?" She glanced at him, tears in her eyes. "What if that's not enough?"

SMOOTHING THE RED DRESS over her hips, Renita eyed herself critically in the full-length mirror. Between the Spanx underwear and sucking in her gut, her stomach was almost flat. Oh, who was she kidding? It curved outward.

Taking a few steps away from the mirror, she glanced over her shoulder. Her hips were still big enough to make a statement, but her muscles were tauter, her flesh less inclined to wobble. This dress made the most of her hourglass figure.

She wasn't just a loans manager or a math whiz or a tomboy who liked animals. She was a woman. No one ever seemed to notice that. Tonight everyone would. Well, chaperones, teachers and a school full of teenagers, anyway.

Brett would notice.

By seven she was ready. Hair, nails, makeup, dress

and shoes—*tick*. On the outside, she was as calm as a millpond. On the inside, frogs were leaping.

The bell rang. She opened the door.

Brett wore a dark gray suit and crisp white dress shirt open at the neck. He was clean-shaven, his blond hair gleaming.

He whistled softly. "You look amazing."

"You're not so bad yourself." She picked up her clutch purse from the hall table. "Is Tegan okay with me coming?"

He hesitated a fraction of a second before he said, "She's fine with it."

Right.

Girding herself for another battle with the teen queen, Renita descended the steps. She had a hand on Brett's arm to steady herself in her four-inch heels, her wrap slipping off her bare shoulders. The evening was warm; dusk was settling over the treetops. A single bright star glowed in an indigo sky.

Tegan was in the back of the car, the colorful dress they'd bought together arranged carefully. Her hair was swept into a ponytail, with long strands hanging on either side of her oval chin. She clenched her hands tightly in her lap.

"You look lovely," Renita told her as she climbed into the front passenger seat.

"Thanks," Tegan replied. A beat passed before she added, "You do, too."

The pause was just long enough to take the shine off the compliment and to cause an awkward silence to settle over the car. Renita tried not to take it personally. She was the adult here, after all.

The brightly lit school gymnasium was decorated with balloons and streamers. A DJ was setting up his sound equipment on the stage, flanked by speakers. Girls and boys clustered at the edges and crowded around tables loaded with soft drinks and finger food. Teachers and parents dotted the gym. Brett introduced Renita to the principal, Blair Nicholson, and they picked up their ID badges from a table near the door.

"Are you going to go find Amy?" Brett asked his daughter.

Tegan shrank closer to his side. "Maybe later."

Renita met Brett's gaze over the top of Tegan's head, her eyebrows raised. *What's going on?*

He made a slight movement of his head, mouthing the word *nervous*.

"Whatever you do, don't embarrass me, okay, Dad?" Tegan said.

"How could I do that?" Brett demanded.

"By dancing weirdly or singing along to the music."

Renita glanced around. "What are we supposed to do as chaperones?"

"The information sheet said our job is to circulate, patrol the halls now and then," Brett explained. "Make sure kids aren't drinking or doing drugs, that there aren't any fights and no one's making out behind the bleachers."

"Do we get to dance?" Renita asked.

"Sure, as long as we don't look—" he winked at Tegan and waggled his fingers "—weird."

"Dad!" Tegan groaned. "You're doing it now."

"Look, there's Oliver," Renita said, seeing a blond, curly head in a group of boys. She waved across the room. "Hey, Olly. Over here."

"Oh, my God." Tegan buried her face in her dad's jacket. "I'm going to die."

Oliver saw Renita and his cheeks burned crimson. Dutifully, he broke away from his mates to come and say hello. Then he spotted Brett and his footsteps quickened. "Hey, Renita. Tegan." With a worshipful smile, he said to Brett, "Hey."

"This is my dad," Tegan mumbled.

On stage, the DJ tested the microphone by saying a few words of welcome.

"Nice to meet you, Oliver," Brett said, shaking the boy's hand. "I understand you're into football."

"I'm a big supporter of Collingwood. It's so cool that you're living in Summerside."

"Thanks for the welcome," Brett replied. "Drop in to the gym. Tegan's usually there after school. And bring your exercise gear. The first visit is free."

"Cool." Oliver shuffled his feet. "Uh, Tegan said you'd show me your Brownlow Medal. I mean, if that's okay."

Tegan's gaze dropped to the floor. She seemed to shrink into herself.

Renita was trying to think of a diversion when, to her surprise, Brett replied easily, "Sure. Anytime."

Tegan stared at her father.

"Cool!" Oliver nodded and grinned.

Up on the stage the DJ put on the first disc, and Amy Winehouse's sultry vocals blared from the speakers. Renita cleared her throat and sent Oliver a meaningful glance.

Her nephew looked blank, then light dawned. "Oh, right." He stuck his hands in the back pockets of his skinny jeans. "Uh, Tegan, do you want to dance?"

The girl hesitated, clearly still worried about the medal.

"It'll be all right," Brett said.

Smiling shyly, his daughter turned to Oliver. "Okay."

Renita watched the young couple merge onto the dance floor. "Why on earth did you tell Olly you'd show him your medal?"

"Because I'm an idiot. Where can we get a drink?" Brett glanced around for the refreshments table.

"Forget it. Soda isn't going to soothe those nerves. Do you still have the medal? Have you changed your mind about selling it?"

"I can't change my mind. I've already ordered the equipment."

"Then why?" Renita stared at him in disbelief.

"I may not be the best parent, but I couldn't watch my daughter crash and burn. Not when she's already having trouble making friends."

"What are you going to do?"

"I haven't got a clue." He shook his head. "Did you tell Oliver to ask her to dance?"

"I probably shouldn't have interfered," Renita said, watching the kids on the dance floor. Bluesy brass music rose above the thudding of dozens of feet. She'd never been to a dance, but she knew what it was like to be unsure of herself.

"I'm glad you did.... Oliver isn't going to just forget about the Brownlow Medal, is he?"

"Not a chance," Renita replied. "I'll have a quiet word with him."

"No, I'll do it." Brett blew out a heavy sigh. "Later. First I'll let Tegan have her night."

Among the teachers, Renita recognized Jack's friend Glenn, a tall, fit man with close-cropped red hair, and waved. When he wandered over she introduced him to Brett. "Glenn teaches phys ed."

"It'd be great if you could give the boys a workshop in Aussie rules football sometime," Glenn said.

The men started talking sports. Renita saw someone else she knew and slipped away to say hello. When she turned around again, Brett was surrounded by a circle of admirers. She grabbed a bottle of mineral water and circulated the floor. She spotted Tegan standing with Oliver and a group of teens. The girl was chatting and smiling, to all appearances having a good time. Renita caught her eye and gave her a thumbs-up. Tegan pretended not to see.

"Here's a golden oldie for all those who love a

great ballad," the DJ said, leaning into the microphone as he dropped a disc on the player.

A hand touched her arm. She turned to see Brett.

When he leaned close and said in her ear, "Would you like to dance?" her stomach fluttered and she caught her breath.

Years ago he'd hurt her so badly she'd cried herself to sleep. Now her pulse quickened as she stepped into his arms. His spicy masculine scent made her almost light-headed. One hand rested in the small of her back, his other palm pressed against hers.

She didn't want this. Yet she couldn't have broken away if her life depended on it. Her eyes drifted closed. She rested her head on his shoulder, feeling the solid strength of his arms and chest.

"Er, Renita?"

"Hmm?" she sighed dreamily.

"Are you dancing or just shuffling your feet?"

She jerked back, heat climbing her neck. "The kids are shuffling, too."

"Because they don't know any better."

"I never learned to dance."

"This is a box step. It's pretty easy."

She glanced up and saw he wasn't ridiculing her. "Show me."

Hands clasped, he drew her close again. "Back, side, together," he murmured in her ear, to hide the fact he was teaching her. "Forward, side, together."

His grip tightened as he led her into a turn at the

corner of the dance floor. "It's nice to know I can teach you something."

She bet there were a lot of things he could teach her. "I'm surprised I never saw you on *Dancing with the Stars*."

"I was asked but…" He made a face, shrugged. "I didn't want to go the route of so many ex-athletes and minor media personalities—being trotted out for red carpet events, variety shows and talk show panels."

"Doesn't Summerside seem tame after the city?"

"I wanted a normal life, for me and for Tegan."

The song ended. A faster number came on.

"Let's go check out the school," Brett said. "Visit our old lockers."

"That'll be fun." *Not.* Renita hid her reluctance and followed him out of the gym, into the wide empty corridor.

"What about you?" Brett said as they walked. "Don't you hanker after the bright lights?"

"Been there, done that. I lived in Melbourne while going to university and working. Then I traveled overseas for a job in London. I got homesick for Summerside, for my family." Renita peered through the glass-paneled door of her old history classroom. It looked the same as it had fifteen years ago.

"Did you go to the tenth reunion?" Brett asked. "I don't recall seeing you there."

"I was still in London."

They wandered past the office and the trophy case

where Brett's photo, as captain of the football team, was displayed next to a silver cup. Past the arts wing and the home economics room.

She didn't know how they ended up in the hallway outside the boys' locker room—she'd been trying to avoid the area—but she must have forgotten the layout of the school. They turned a corner and she found herself standing in the exact spot where she'd invited Brett to the dance and he'd turned her down.

The same odor of sweaty gym socks pervaded the hall. There was the notice board with the list of names for the sports teams and the schedule of practice. The pennants on the wall, a poster for an upcoming football game between Summerside and Frankston.

Renita stopped, overcome by a rush of shame, hurt, anger. "Let's get out of here."

"Not yet." Brett lifted his hand and brushed her cheek with his knuckles.

She held her breath as he slowly lowered his head. His lips were gentle at first, nipping at the edges of her mouth while his breath mingled with hers. Renita placed a hand flat on his chest, feeling the beat of his heart. She rose up on tiptoe, lifting herself into his kiss, her arms twined around his neck.

She used to dream about what it would feel like to kiss Brett. Now she knew. *Wonderful,* she told herself. And yet... She realized she was trying to convince herself it was true. As amazing a kisser as Brett was, something didn't feel right.

His arms tightened around her. She could feel him hard against her. But she wasn't engaged.

Gently, she pushed him away.

"What's wrong?" he asked.

"You're very…skillful. But your kiss lacked…I don't know…sincerity."

"Ouch! I thought maybe I could make up for…" He trailed off, grimacing. "Dumb, I know."

Renita slowly spun on her high heels, taking in the scene. "This whole setup, the high school dance, the dress… I thought I would make this triumphant return on the arm of my high school crush." She faced him and stopped. "You can't go back."

"So you had a crush on me," he said.

She nodded. "But I'm over it. I truly am."

Brett's hands slid up her bare arms, making her shiver.

Suddenly Renita was very much engaged. What she hadn't said was that she was falling for him again. But it was different this time.

Deeper, stronger. Scarier.

CHAPTER TEN

THIS IS A MISTAKE, she thought as she followed Brett upstairs to his bedroom, her hand trailing along the sleek wood banister. Tegan was staying overnight at Amy's house with some of their classmates. It had been a last-minute invitation.

Nothing really had changed. He was still the golden boy. He'd hurt her once by rejecting her invitation to a dance. If she made love with him and then he rejected her again... How much more painful would that be?

Brett turned on a lamp. A soft golden glow illuminated a spacious room containing a king-size bed, a couple of club chairs, a small coffee table and a writing desk.

"You've got enough room to swing a kangaroo in here," Renita said, padding across the plush champagne carpet. "You need more furniture. Plants. Something."

Brett flung his jacket over one of the club chairs. "Would you like a drink?"

Nervous, she spun away from him.

Floor-to-ceiling windows and sliding glass doors

ran the length of the house, overlooking the bay. She pushed open a door and went through it onto the balcony. The lights of Melbourne and the seaside suburbs twinkled around the long sweeping curve of the bay.

Brett came outside and put his arms around her waist from behind. His voice rumbled next to her ear as he said, "Don't be nervous."

Renita turned in his arms to face him. "I'm not sure I'm ready for this. I'm not sure *we're* ready."

He didn't argue. Instead, he drew her back inside the room and led her in a box step, humming the tune they'd danced to earlier.

Gradually his feet slowed. He brushed her mouth with kisses that tantalized and teased her. Her heart thumping, she undid the top buttons of his shirt and slid a hand inside. His skin was warm from the summer evening and the dancing. A scattering of blond chest hair glinted in the glow of the bedside lamp as she ran her fingers over his muscular chest. This was Brett she was touching.

He removed his shirt then undid the catch on the halter. The top slid down, baring her breasts. He released his breath in a soft sigh that raised goose bumps and puckered her nipples.

Then his hands and mouth seemed to be everywhere at once. He captured a nipple between his teeth with a delicate pressure that brought her up on her toes, then tickled and sucked till her knees went weak from the pulling sensation inside her.

With her fingers she traced the hard, defined muscles of his arms. His skin was hot, burning up. Their breathing quickened as they loosened the rest of their clothes and dropped them to the floor in a tangle. Naked bodies bumped, pressed, twined.

Holding her gaze again, Brett danced her over to the bed, making her laugh with a giddy exhilaration. The backs of her legs hit the mattress and she sat abruptly, pulling him down on top of her.

Her laughter faded as she acknowledged that her body was still soft and plump despite the hours of running and gym work. In comparison, his body was unbelievably hard, and scarred from football.

He rolled, taking her with him so they lay on their sides, facing each other. "What is it? What are you thinking?"

Stretching out a finger, she traced the sharp angle at the corner of his mouth. "Would you—" Her voice cracked and she had to take a deep breath and begin again. "Would you have invited me into your bed if I hadn't lost weight, ditched the glasses and glammed up?"

He didn't speak for what seemed like ages. Finally he looked her in the eye and said with devastating honesty, "Probably not."

His reply caused an actual physical pain in her chest. Well, she'd asked for it. "You're being truthful. I appreciate that."

"I'm not used to being turned down," he added. "I don't take rejection well."

She blinked, confused. "I don't understand. Why do you think *I'd* have rejected *you?*"

"That first day in your office, you wouldn't talk about anything personal. No matter how hard I tried, you didn't want to admit that we'd been friends. If I'd come on to you, how do you think that would have turned out? You wouldn't have believed I was sincere, not for a second."

She thought about that. "You've got a point, I suppose."

"I didn't used to think you were attractive," he admitted. "Maybe I asked you out because of the way you look now. Maybe it's also because I've gotten to know you better. You've changed in other ways, too. Confidence is just as attractive as beauty."

Renita considered that. In a way, he was paying her a compliment in not flattering her falsely.

"Roll over," he said, having Renita face the reflection of the two of them in the wardrobe mirrors. "What do you see?"

Herself lying in front of him, naked and vulnerable. She was so used to being critical of her body. She tried to look past that and see herself objectively. She was red-cheeked, all curves. "I think I'm sexy."

His voice vibrated next to her ear. "I do, too."

His long fingers traveled the swell of her hip, dipped to her waist and slid up to cup her breast. Slowly he began to massage her, squeezing her nipple lightly between his fingers. She could feel the rasp of his jaw on her cheek and the hard jut of his erection against her butt.

He nudged his penis between her legs, pushing in, then easing out, teasing her, the delicious friction releasing a flood of moisture. Renita couldn't tear her eyes away from the sight of him touching her. Squeezing her nipples, drifting lower to the juncture of her thighs and stroking her—building an aching hollow inside that she longed to have him fill.

Now fully aroused, she turned away from the mirror toward Brett. She lifted her mouth to his, her throat thick with emotion. Rolling over, she grabbed his hips and, as he thrust into her, her anxieties evaporated in the heat of his gaze.

"WE'VE GOT LEFTOVER spaghetti and meatballs, sliced turkey, cheese, eggs…." Brett, his head in the fridge, handed the various items out to Renita. "Pickles, apples…"

"Stop," she said, laughing, her arms full of food. "I'll have some spaghetti. It's not on my diet, but I reckon I've burned off a few calories tonight."

Grinning, he put the container in the microwave.

"Dancing," she said, blushing. She lounged against the opposite counter of the U-shaped kitchen, looking cute in his bathrobe, her brown hair tousled.

While the food heated she chatted about the evening—the teachers, teenage fashion, music. She seemed more relaxed than usual, as if she finally trusted him.

Amber or any of the other footy groupies would have taken it for granted that they were hot. After years of shallow relationships, women with fake boobs, false eyelashes, phony tans, hair extensions, acrylic nails, Botox to their foreheads, collagen-injected lips…he was exhausted. In contrast, Renita's unadorned natural beauty was—

"…Olly seems to like Tegan as much as she likes him."

That brought Brett to the present. "What do you know about him? This is the first boy Tegan's shown an interest in."

"He's Dr. Sienna Maxwell's son, soon to be my brother Jack's stepson," Renita explained. "Oliver's a good kid. Smart, polite, nice. Tegan could do a lot worse."

"She's only thirteen," Brett said, taking hold of Renita's lapels and running his thumbs over the rough nap of the navy terry cloth robe.

"I'm sure it's innocent."

"It better be." He pulled her close for a lingering kiss.

The microwave beeped. Brett brought out the food, dividing it onto two plates. "Can you eat this much?"

"Oh, yes. I didn't have dinner."

"Really? Why not?" He carried the plates across the open plan kitchen/family room to the round glass table in the breakfast nook.

"I had a date with Brett O'Connor," Renita said,

pulling out a wicker chair to sit. "I was way too nervous to eat."

Brett went back to the kitchen for glasses of water. "I hope he lived up to your expectations."

"Not bad." Grinning, she twirled her fork into the pasta.

He pretended to wince. "I thought for once you'd give me a good score."

Brett carried their drinks down on the table, then went back to the counter for his cell phone. "Go ahead and start. I should check my voice mail in case Tegan had any problems."

He clicked a few buttons and sure enough there was a message. But it wasn't from Tegan. It was from Simon Toltz. "Excuse me," he said to Renita and walked away a few paces to listen.

Bad news, Simon had said. *The deal has fallen through. Back to square one. Not to worry. I've already put more feelers out.*

Not to worry? Brett had ordered the equipment and paid a thirty thousand dollar deposit!

"Is it Tegan?" Renita asked. "You've gone pale."

"No, it's not Tegan." He turned the phone off. Sitting back down at the table, he pushed his plate away. He hadn't just lost his appetite, he felt sick. "The sale of my Brownlow Medal fell through."

Renita stopped twirling pasta and dropped her fork on the plate. "Oh, my God." She stared at him. "The equipment you ordered."

He nodded, still stunned.

"Can you return it?"

"I don't know." He speared his hands through his hair, unable to think.

"Why couldn't you have waited until you actually had the money in hand before you placed your order?" Renita pushed away her unfinished plate of food.

"Easy to say in hindsight."

"*No.* It's obviously the most sensible course of action." She frowned, thinking a moment. "I'll lend you the money."

"You mean, a bank loan?" he asked, hope rising.

"No, a personal loan. From me." She seemed eager to help. "I could take out a second mortgage on my house—"

"Out of the question." Brett slapped a hand on the table. He got to his feet and pushed his chair back. "I can't take that kind of money from you."

"Why not, if we're…" She trailed off uncertainly.

"Because it would taint our relationship." Hell, they'd only slept together once. "I would look like an opportunistic sleaze."

She stared at him then said slowly, "Only if you knew about the offer falling through before you asked me to stay overnight."

He stared back at her, hard. Could she really think that of him? "You saw me take the message just now."

Renita picked up a fork. Dropped it again. "You're

right. I'm sorry." There was the slightest edge to her voice.

"*Thank* you, though," he said. "It's a generous offer. But you've clearly made it without thinking."

"Sure." With a soft sigh, she rose. "I'd better go."

"Now?" He glanced at the clock. "It's nearly one in the morning. I assumed you would stay—"

"Brett, come on," she said. "After the conversation we just had, can you honestly see us going back to bed together?"

He opened his mouth to disagree but then his shoulders slumped. She was right.

"WHAT HAPPENED?" Brett had waited as patiently as he could until it was a decent hour that Sunday morning to ring Simon Toltz. At nine o'clock sharp he'd dialed the dealer's number.

"Apparently the sale was contingent on the buyer's remortgaging his house," Simon explained, adding drily, "When his wife found out he was spending nearly two hundred grand for a Brownlow Medal she kicked up a fuss. Some people have no sense of history."

Brett was ready to tear his hair out by the roots. "What about the next bidder? Can you call him and see if he's still interested?"

"I already have. When your medal went off the market he invested in a pine plantation. The next one below that was prepared to bid only $100,000."

"That's not enough," Brett said.

"I presumed not, so I didn't contact him. I am, however, making another round of inquiries."

"Okay." He sighed. "Let me know if anything happens."

First thing Monday morning Brett called the sporting goods company in Perth he'd ordered from, and asked to speak to someone in accounts. He was put through to Rick, a young man who, judging by his nasal voice, had a summer cold.

"Brett O'Connor here," he said. "I ordered some gym equipment last week."

"I remember," Rick said. "Biggest order I've taken, and I've worked here for nearly six years. You should have seen the office when we got your email. Everyone running around, checking stock, figuring out if we could fill it. It was a red letter day at West Coast Sports, let me tell you." He sniffed. "What can I do for you?"

"I'd like to cancel the order."

Silence. "You...want to *cancel* the order?"

"Correct."

"Hold on, let me check your account." Rick coughed and sneezed, and in the background Brett heard computer keys. "Say, are you *the* Brett O'Connor, the football player?"

"Yep. So can I cancel?"

"We don't have a returns policy," Rick said. More clicking in the background. "You would lose your deposit."

Brett rubbed his hand along his jaw. He couldn't afford to do that. "Can you delay the order, or send it out in smaller installments?"

"Nope." Rick blew his nose.

"I've run into a cash flow problem," Brett explained. "I want the equipment, just not all at once."

"I understand. Trouble is, the order has already been shipped."

"Oh, no." Brett covered his face with his hand.

"You asked us to expedite it. It's on its way by truck. Should get to Melbourne the day after tomorrow, cash on delivery."

"You can't recall it?"

"Afraid not." Rick sniffed.

"I can't pay for it," Brett said bluntly. "Not right away."

Another silence. "Let me talk to my manager. Can you hold?"

Brett paced the kitchen while he waited. He glanced at his watch. He should be at the gym right now. And he'd planned to stop by Steve's house to check on him. Although he didn't know why he bothered sometimes. The man didn't seem to appreciate his efforts. If it wasn't for Renita—

"Brett, you there?" Rick said. "My manager says that since you've paid a deposit—and frankly, since you're Brett O'Connor—he'll waive the requirement for cash on delivery. But you'll need to make an installment within fifteen days, with the balance due in thirty. And there'll be interest charged for every day over the delivery date."

The terms were tough, but they gave him breathing space. "Thanks, Rick. That's a load off my mind."

"I'm a big fan of yours. And so is my boss," Rick said with a wheezing cough. "I doubt he'd do that for just anyone."

"I appreciate the vote of confidence." Brett paused. "Hypothetically speaking, what would happen if the fifteen days were up and I couldn't pay the installment?"

"The order would be repossessed, you'd lose your deposit and have to pay shipping costs."

Spelling the end of the Brett O'Connor Fitness Center.

"Is that likely to happen?" Rick sounded worried.

"No, not a problem," Brett said heartily. "I'll have the money."

WASN'T IT POLITE to call someone after spending the night together? Renita wondered as she drove home from work on Monday. Even though they hadn't parted on the best of terms that night, she hadn't thought their relationship would be *damaged*. She'd phoned Brett twice. Not a word back. If nothing else, she wanted to know if he'd found another buyer for his medal.

She pulled into her driveway and parked in the carport. Through the open car window she could hear

Frankie squawk at the familiar sound of her engine. She was on her way out back through the gate to say hello to him when the phone started ringing. She hurried inside, racing down the hall to the kitchen.

"Hello?" she said breathlessly.

"Did I get you in from the garden?" Hetty asked. "Sorry, darling."

"Where are you?" Renita demanded, disappointed that it wasn't Brett. "Have you come home?"

"I'm still in Queensland," her mother said. "I've enrolled in a new program, training to be a yoga instructor."

Renita bit her tongue. Hetty was in great shape, and fifty-five wasn't old. Why shouldn't she start a new career? "That's great, Mother. But Dad misses you terribly."

"Darling, I'm not a child. You don't have to make things up. He can't miss me very much if he's stepping out on a Saturday night—"

"Whoa, hold on." Renita dropped her purse and keys on the kitchen counter and kicked off her shoes. Padding over to the fridge for a glass of water, she asked, "What do you mean, 'stepping out'?"

"I called home to find out how Smedley was. Steve could barely spare me five minutes. He said he was on his way out for the evening. Didn't say where, but he was practically buzzing with excitement."

"Maybe he was heading to Jack's for dinner," Renita suggested. "I know he had a few people around this weekend. That's nothing unusual."

"I called Jack. Steve wasn't there. Not expected, either."

Renita couldn't contain her resentment. "You left him. Why do you care what he does?" It was all very well for Hetty to run off to Queensland, but she'd abandoned Steve when he was sick and depressed.

"He's still my husband," her mother said with quiet dignity.

"Does that mean you're not separating?"

Hetty hesitated. "I may have been hasty." She took a shaky breath. "Something's going on. I want to know what."

Oh, God, Renita thought. What if her stolid, conservative father had taken Brett's pep talk to heart and started clubbing? Seeing other women? "Maybe he got together with some of his mates from the Men's Shed."

"He's never done that before. He spends hours there during the day, but always comes home to eat. Then he watches TV all evening. Steve is a creature of habit."

"People can change," Renita pointed out. "You did."

"Could you please find out what's happening?" Hetty asked. "I'm starting my training tomorrow. I don't want my focus weakened by worrying about Steve."

"If you're worried, why don't you come back and check on him yourself?"

"Renita."

"Oh, all right." She sighed. "I'll go around after dinner and see what I can find out."

She hung up, then noticed that the red light on the answering machine was blinking, and pressed Play.

"Hey, Renita." Brett sounded rushed and harried. "Sorry I haven't returned your calls. I've been really busy. The gym will be closed for a couple of days. The new equipment is arriving. We'll have to cancel your personal training. Talk soon."

A beep signaled the end of the message.

Renita stared at the telephone. Talk about abrupt. Hetty wasn't the only one who wanted to know what was going on.

CHAPTER ELEVEN

RENITA GAVE A COURTESY knock, then turned the handle to walk in, as she always did. Her father's door was locked. The curtains were drawn, but no lights were on. Inside, Smedley began to bark in his deep voice, no doubt under the illusion that he was a German shepherd.

She went around to peer over the fence into the backyard.

Empty.

It was Tuesday. He obviously hadn't taken Smedley for a walk. Where would he go midweek? It was a little late for grocery shopping—

"Are you looking for your father?" Mrs. Lockhart, the elderly woman next door, was in her garden pruning her roses in the fading light. A Maltese terrier with a pink bow between her ears was flopped on the grass.

Renita walked across the lawn to talk over the low fence. "Do you know where he is?"

Mrs. Lockhart dropped a thorny stem into the plastic tub at her feet and pushed back a strand of gray hair with her wrist. "He said he was going to the library."

"The library?" Renita blinked. Her father subscribed to *Agricultural Digest* magazine, but he wasn't what she'd call a reader.

"He was putting out the rubbish bins earlier and we got to talking. I mentioned my overdue books and he offered to return them for me, since he was going there, anyway." Tilting her head, she snipped off another dead blossom. "The library shuts at eight."

Renita glanced at her watch. It was eight-thirty. The trip home from the library shouldn't take more than five or ten minutes.

"Okay. Well, thanks." She started back to her car.

"I notice your mother's still away." Mrs. Lockhart called.

Busybody. "She's in Queensland training for a new job," Renita said. "She'll be back soon."

Before the woman could ask more questions, Renita got in her car and drove around the corner. She parked, then called her dad on his cell phone. No answer. That wasn't unusual. He'd only bought the phone a few months ago, after his emergency trip to the hospital. Half the time he forgot to turn it on.

Renita carried on to the library, even though she figured it was a waste of time. The main part of the building was dark, and through the big windows she couldn't see anyone among the stacks. But a meeting room at the front was lit and below the pulled-down blinds she could see the shoes of people who were moving around.

Something was going on in there, but at least they appeared to be fully clothed. Her father hadn't joined Swingers in the Suburbs.

The automatic doors to the building opened as she approached, and she went in. Renita peered around the half-open door to the meeting room. Tables arranged in a U shape facing a lectern were occupied by men and women ranging in age from twenty to sixty plus. Standing at the lectern was a smartly dressed woman in her early fifties. Over her chin-length blond hair she wore a multicolored jester cap, complete with bells that jingled as she moved.

What the—

Then Renita noticed that everyone wore a hat of some type. Baseball caps, sun hats…there was even a top hat and a sombrero. Steve wore the battered felt hat he used around the farm. He'd pinned a jaunty green-and-yellow rosella feather to the band.

What on earth had her father gotten mixed up in?

The blonde in the jester hat began to tell the group a story about her car breaking down at night on the freeway. Just as she got to the point where a Good Samaritan stopped to help her, she broke off and gestured to the man at the end of the table. He rose and continued the story, saying how relieved he was that help had arrived. That is, until the car door opened— and a tall pale man in a long black cape emerged.

Renita's thoughts immediately flew to vampires, and she must have made a noise. The moderator's eyes flicked to the door and Renita shrank back. She ought to leave, but at that moment her dad got heavily to his feet. He planted his fingers on the table and stood for a moment with his head down.

"Uh…" he began. "I…uh…"

Renita cringed. To say he wasn't good at public speaking would be a massive understatement. She still recalled his clumsy attempt to say a few words at his and Hetty's twenty-fifth wedding anniversary.

"The man in the cape…uh…smiled." Steve stumbled over the words. "In the streetlight I could see his teeth were pointed. And sharp. I, uh, went to the trunk. That's right. Where I kept my toolbox. I pretended I was getting a jack for the flat tire. Then I, um, pulled out the thing I carry in case of emergencies—a wooden stake."

Laughter erupted. The moderator tapped her gavel to signal Steve's turn was over. With a relieved grin he sat down, and the next person continued the story. Renita listened as the vampire was killed and a werewolf arrived to hijack the repaired car, kidnapping the hapless driver and taking him to a mountain hideout, where he was rescued by helicopter.…

And on it went, sometimes fantastical, sometimes mundane, depending on who was making up that segment of the story. There didn't seem to be any point to the exercise that Renita could see, but these people were clearly having fun. She marveled as Steve enjoyed some fresh piece of nonsense.

The story had now gone around the circle, and finished to enthusiastic applause. Renita was about to sneak away when the MC said, "Come in, whoever's lurking out there. Join us, please. Visitors are welcome at Toastmasters."

All heads turned in her direction. She had no choice but to step inside.

"Sorry. I was just…" *Looking for my father.* "I saw the lights and I thought the library might be open," she finished lamely.

She met Steve's gaze and smiled. Then she ducked out.

Toastmasters, of all things. Before she'd reached her car she'd texted the news to Lexie and Jack. Sliding into the driver's seat, she began to call Hetty. Then she stopped.

Thoughtfully, she started the car and drove home.

The gym will be closed for two days due to a major refurbishment. Sorry for the inconvenience.

Brett hit Send on the mass email to gym members. Then he sent the same message via text to cell phones.

The truck containing the exercise machines had arrived early that afternoon from Perth. For hours workmen in overalls had brought in crate after crate through the propped-open doors.

A burly black-haired man wheeling a dolly lifted his chin. "Where do you want this one, mate?"

"Through there." Brett pointed to the cardio room.

The workers Brett had hired were dismantling and removing the old exercise machines. Janet and Matt helped make sure everything ended up in the right location, and programmed each new machine as it was installed.

"This is fantastic," Janet gushed as she escorted a fleet of stationary bicycles to the spin room. "You're a genius to get this stuff delivered in time for the grand opening."

Oh, yeah, he was a genius all right. The gym was finally starting to resemble the vision in his head. But how was he going to pay for it?

"Did you get the flyers sent to the printers?" he asked.

She nodded. "They'll be delivered to the distributor by the end of the week."

The day passed in a blur of activity and the stack of wooden crates in the parking lot next to the shipping container mounted. The three of them worked without letup, breaking only for a quick sandwich from the deli.

Brett called Tegan at three to tell her to go directly home or to her grandparents' house. The gym was no place for homework.

Around dinnertime he was stripping plastic off a new cross-country ski machine. The workmen had left, and Janet and Matt had gone into the village to get more food.

"Brett!" Renita came through the open doors. She was in her gym gear, dressed for a workout. "So the new equipment arrived. I had to come down and see for myself." Although her voice was bright, her manner was strained and she kept her distance.

He crumpled the stripped-off plastic into a ball, hardly able to look her in the face. He'd wanted to show her he could be a success at business, and for her to be pleased his gym was properly fitted out, confident he could take care of the cost.

"I take it you couldn't cancel the order," Renita said, glancing around the cardio room at the new machines.

He shook his head. "I've got fifteen days to come up with the rest of the money."

"Any more nibbles on your medal?"

"Nope." He was so ashamed he walked out of the room just to get away from her. Toltz had told him the market had dried up.

"Bummer," she said, following him. "What's going to happen?"

What kind of a dumb question was that? "I'm going to get the money."

"How?" she persisted.

"I just will, okay?" he snapped. He wanted her

admiration and respect, not her sympathy. And disapproval.

"My offer still stands…."

And he sure as hell didn't want her help. "No!"

She jerked back as if he'd slapped her. "Okay. Fine." Hands up, she backed off. "You're busy. Since I can't train I'll go for a run."

"Renita," he called. But his appeal was half-hearted.

She was already out the door, halfway to her car.

RENITA STALKED OUT OF the gym. The tears burning the backs of her eyelids vaporized in the heat of her growing anger. Fine! He could crash and burn for all she cared. He'd gone against her professional advice. He deserved everything he got.

Fumbling for her car keys, she unlocked the door and got in. Her hands shook as she gripped the steering wheel. She left the parking lot and turned off the main drag at the road to her father's house. She thumped the wheel with her fist. She'd tried to be supportive but now she was furious with him.

How could Brett have placed that order, not knowing if he'd be able to pay for it? So risky. And what a price to pay. His *Brownlow Medal*. He would never get that back once it was gone.

And what if a new buyer wasn't willing to pay the

amount Brett needed? Surely he'd thought of that? If he had to return the equipment, that would be the end of the gym, the end of his dream.

She turned into Steve's driveway and parked. The drapes were open. Smedley barked at her, his front paws up against the window.

Her father opened the door before she could knock. He was in his undershirt and a pair of not very clean trousers, but at least his hair appeared to be washed.

"Hey, Dad." She was relieved to catch him at home so she wouldn't have to be alone. "Want to go for a run?" With a start she realized she also craved the feel-good high that came with a hard workout.

"Oh, I guess so," he grumbled. "Brett said he'd be on my case if I didn't do something while the gym was closed."

Her mouth firmed at the mention of his name. She wasn't in the mood to hear about the good things he'd done. "I understand he's been coming around."

"He brought a load of fresh veggies yesterday. He got me making some fool stir-fry dish like your mother cooks. Hang on a tick, I'll go change." Steve headed to his bedroom.

Renita stooped to pat Smedley, then, pushing Brett from her thoughts, wandered through the living room. She was not spying for her mother; she was just concerned about how her father was getting along.

The house still had a bachelor pad look—a beer

bottle left on the side table, sports magazines strewn over the couch. But overall, the place was reasonably clean and tidy.

She ducked her head into the hall—her father hadn't come out of his room—then went to the kitchen and opened the fridge. Fresh fruit, potatoes, green vegetables, lamb chops. Pretty impressive for someone not used to cooking for himself.

"Brett brought all that." In sports socks, Steve made no sound on the tile floor as he came in. He wore a navy T-shirt and shorts. "You hungry?"

"No." She shut the fridge. "I was just…looking for a bottle of water. I forgot to bring one."

"I fill mine from the tap," Steve said. "It's cheaper." He opened a cupboard to retrieve a couple of reusable water bottles.

Renita drove them to the small gravel parking area on Cliff Road. She wanted to see if she could handle this route without Brett urging her on. After performing a few stretches she and her dad set off.

"You should have joined us at the Toastmasters meeting the other night," Steve said as they began to jog slowly up the first hill.

"I didn't come prepared for anything like that." Renita could have gone faster, but kept pace with her father.

"What were you doing there then?" he asked.

"Honestly? Mum wanted to know how you were, what you were doing," she replied. "I stopped by the

house and your neighbor mentioned you'd gone to the
library." She glanced at him. "What made you join
Toastmasters?"

"Ray, one of the guys at the Men's Shed, dragged
me along to a meeting after I told him I was nervous
about giving a speech at my son's wedding reception.
It's kind of fun," Steve admitted grudgingly.

"I could see that. That was some crazy story. Who
knew you had such an imagination?"

"I'm giving my icebreaker speech next week.
That's where I tell the group about myself. You could
come as a guest."

"Maybe I will." She sensed he would appreciate
the moral support. And she was curious about this
unexpected new side to her father. "I might learn
something."

As they jogged past Brett's house, Renita glanced
through the wrought-iron gate, even though she knew
he wasn't there. Her frustration must have shown
because Steve asked, "What's wrong? Did Brett do
something to upset you?"

"You wouldn't believe what he did, Daddy." She
proceeded to tell the whole story, omitting the fact
that she'd slept with the man. Her sex life was none
of her father's business, and she was pretty sure he
wouldn't want to know. "Now he's scared and cover-
ing his fear with bravado. He won't let me help. He
won't even talk to me."

He couldn't even look her in the eye. He'd shut
her out. That's what hurt. She was still upset but her

anger had dissolved. She was back to just wanting to help him.

"It would be a shame if he lost the gym over this," Steve said. He paused. "By help him, do you mean financially?"

"I've offered him a personal loan. He wouldn't—" She broke off, a thought striking her. "*I* could buy his Brownlow Medal."

"You!" Steve cocked one eyebrow. "Why would you do that?"

"Why not? It's an investment," she said defensively.

They'd come to the cul-de-sac. Traversing the trail down the cliff put an end to their conversation. Renita waited on the beach for Steve, whose joints didn't take as kindly to the uneven steep slope. Together they jogged slowly across the sand to where it was firmer, near the water.

"Be practical, Renita. Would you even have enough money to buy his Brownlow?" Steve asked, picking up their conversation where they'd left off.

"For years I've been putting every penny I've earned into paying off my mortgage." She thought furiously. "If I refinanced, I'd have enough, just."

"A Brownlow Medal isn't something you'd normally buy," Steve said. "Brett will see it as a loan in disguise. What makes you think he'll accept your money?"

"He can't know I'm buying the medal. I'll somehow find out who the dealer is and do it anonymously."

Steve stopped jogging. "Renita. Are you in love with him?"

"No, I just…" She sucked in a breath. "I've gotten to know him, Dad. He's got faults but so does everyone. He cares about people. Look what he's done for you. He didn't have to go to so much trouble. I think, maybe, he did it partly for me."

"I don't know what his motives are," Steve said gruffly. "It bothers me that he's going to hurt you all over again."

"He won't," Renita said. But even as she spoke tears welled in her eyes.

"Here you are, all upset. He's doing it already." Steve found a handkerchief in his pocket and gave it to her. "Brett's a decent guy in many respects. But I don't trust him with my daughter. He's a footy player. Those guys go through women like tissues."

"He needs my help," she said, blotting her eyes. "He's too proud to accept it."

"Brett ordered the equipment before he had the cash. It doesn't mean *you* should throw away your hard-earned savings. You've been careful with your money, and now he's going to come along and reap the reward? He's the grasshopper and you're the ant. Don't you see how big a difference there is between you two?"

Renita nodded. The tinge of bitterness in her father's voice made her wonder if he was thinking of more than her and Brett. Was he also thinking of himself and Hetty?

As if she'd read his mind, he changed the subject. "How's your mother?"

"She's training to be a yoga instructor."

Steve's expression was guarded. "Did she say when she'd be back?"

Renita shook her head. "Maybe you should go up there. Go get her." When Steve said nothing, she added, "At least call and talk to her."

"Not yet. She needs her space. Besides..." His mouth twisted. "I'm starting to believe I can survive on my own."

"There's surviving and then there's thriving. Could you be happy without Mum?"

"I might not have a choice, so why does that matter?"

"Well, I'm glad you're getting out and doing things."

She *was* glad. But her parents' growing independence from each other was frightening, too. Where did that leave their marriage? For the first time, Renita wondered what Hetty and Steve had been like before they got married. Were their personalities as different back then as hers and Brett's were? Or had they grown apart as they'd gotten older? Without children at home was there anything left to bind them together as a couple?

She wanted a love that would last. All her life she'd believed her parents' marriage was set in stone. Now nothing seemed solid, everything was shifting. As a teenager she'd thought that if only Brett wanted her she couldn't ask for anything more.

Now… Well, now she didn't know what she thought.

THAT EVENING RENITA SAT at her kitchen table with her laptop and logged on to her online bank account to check the status of her mortgage. She'd been paying into it steadily for ten years. By her own—that is, the bank's—guidelines, she calculated she could borrow back a hundred and eighty-five thousand dollars. Which meant she needed another ten thousand. She was saving for a new car, but that would have to wait.

Reaching for the phone, she rang Jack.

"Good evening, brother dear," she sang.

"What do you want?" he asked suspiciously.

No point beating around the bush. Jack always knew when she needed something. "A loan of ten thousand dollars."

"Oh, sure, because I have that much money lying around as pocket change."

Renita explained the situation. "I'll pay you the current rate of interest."

"What are you going to do with the Brownlow Medal once you've got it?" he asked. "Sell it on?"

"No, the whole point is to keep it from leaving Brett's hands. I'll buy it and he can pay off his debts. Then when the gym is a success—" she crossed her fingers "—he can buy the medal back."

"What if he doesn't want to?"

"He will," Renita stated confidently. "You should have seen his face when he told me he'd had to sell it. But if he won't or can't buy it, I can always sell it again."

"You hope. Renita, this is huge. I trust you know what you're doing."

"Save it. I've already had the lecture from Dad. So can you loan me the money?"

"When do you need it?"

"Right away. I don't want to take a chance on someone else buying the medal."

"I can only muster five thousand on short notice."

Renita bit her lip. "Okay, well, that's fantastic, Jack. Every bit helps. Thank you so much."

She still needed five thousand. Lexie never had any money, so there was no point asking her. Renita didn't want to ask her father. He'd made it clear he thought she was wasting her hard-earned cash.

Who then? You didn't go to friends and ask for that kind of money. Not her friends, anyway. They were generous, but most had young families.

Brett's family? She shied away from the idea. She'd met his parents a couple of times over the years. They were lovely people, but not well off. If Brett had thought he could borrow from them he already would have.

On the other hand, while he might not be able to

borrow hundreds of thousands from them, they might be able to part with five thousand.

"I WANTED TO HELP BRETT," Mary said to Renita. "He refused because, well, he's like that." With a work-roughened hand she reached out to touch Renita's fingers across the corner of the glass coffee table. "I'm *so* glad you came to us. We had no idea he was in this much strife."

"You mustn't tell him about this," Renita stressed. "Not ever. He wouldn't accept my help, either." He would hate it if he knew she was going around collecting money on his behalf. She glanced out the window. "You're not expecting him, are you?"

"No, he's at the gym." Mary pulled the gray cat winding around her ankles into her lap, and stroked it absently.

"Couldn't the bank lend him even five thousand?" Hal asked. He leaned forward, his elbows on his knees, a shock of graying blond hair falling over his broad forehead.

"If I were to process a loan on his behalf he would have to sign it, and then he'd want to know what it was for," Renita explained. "Someone else could come forward and buy the medal. He'd be out of debt, but I think it would be better if he had the possibility of getting it back."

"Definitely." Mary nudged her taciturn husband. "The night he won the Brownlow was the proudest moment of our lives, wasn't it, darl'?"

"He's going to know you bought it when you sell it back to him," Hal warned.

"I've thought of that," Renita said. "As his loans officer I'm privy to his financial records. When I figure he can afford it, I'll put it back on the market and tell the dealer to approach Brett first."

"Brett won't like that," Hal said. "It's deceitful."

"I'm not crazy about the plan, either," Renita confessed. "It's risky. But what's the alternative? Seriously. The clock is ticking on this."

Mary glanced anxiously at her husband.

"All right." Hal clapped his meaty hands on his thighs. "We'll do it."

"I'll write this up as a personal loan from you to me, and give you a copy of the repayment schedule, plus interest," Renita said, rising. "Thank you so much."

"No, thank *you*," Mary said, squeezing her hand warmly. "Come with Brett the next time he's here for dinner. We'd love to see you. This is a wonderful thing you're doing for our son."

Renita made a vague promise to return sometime with Brett, and took her leave. There was just one small problem left. Who was the dealer Brett was selling his medal through?

She'd have preferred not to enlist Tegan's help— Brett was unlikely to have confided his money problems to his daughter and he wouldn't appreciate Renita dragging her into it—but Renita couldn't think of anyone else who might have access to the information she needed.

CHAPTER TWELVE

IT WAS LESS THAN two miles from the O'Connor family's older home to Brett's fancy big house, but it might as well have been a world away. Renita rang the doorbell and waited impatiently. She could hear pop music so she knew Tegan was home.

The teen opened the door still wearing her green gingham school uniform and white kneesocks. Her expression turned cool when she saw it was Renita. "Dad's not here."

"I know. I just went past the gym and saw his car in the lot. I want to talk to you." Ungrateful little wretch. Had she forgotten already that Renita had introduced her to Oliver?

Then she noticed the bottle of spray cleaner on the hall table and the rag in Tegan's hand. A bucketful of cleaning products and sponges stood at the foot of the stairs. "Are you doing housework?"

"Who did you *think* does it?"

Renita had imagined Brett employed a cleaning lady. "This is a big house to take care of."

"No kidding." With a show of reluctance Tegan stepped back and let Renita enter.

"I won't stay long." Renita walked through the foyer into the living room. "Did you enjoy the dance last week?"

"It was okay." Tegan crossed to the coffee table and took a hair clip from a pewter dish. She held it out, her other hand planted on her cocked hip. "You left this here that night."

Renita met her resentful gaze with a mixture of exasperation and pity. She made no move to accept the clip. "Tegan, you went to an after party. I didn't take your father's attention away from you that night, did I?"

The teen hunched one shoulder. "No, but—"

"I'm not your enemy," Renita went on. "In fact, I need your help."

Tegan dropped the clip back on the coffee table. "To do what?" she asked warily.

"To get his Brownlow Medal back."

"I still can't believe he sold the medal!" Tegan collapsed into a chair opposite Renita. "He *loved* that thing."

"When people are desperate they're forced into making difficult choices. If I can find out who's handling the sale I might be able to fix it so that your dad gets the money *and* the chance to buy back the medal in the future."

Tegan sat up straighter. "What do you want me to do?"

Renita breathed a small sigh of relief that the girl was willing to set aside her animosity for her father's sake. "It'll be either an auction house or a private dealer. He might have left a business card lying around or a phone number scribbled on a paper."

"You want me to snoop? I don't go into his room when he's not here, much less look around."

"I know it's wrong. Maybe I shouldn't have asked you." Renita twisted her fingers together in her lap. She'd taken too big a risk coming here. If Tegan told her father…

"It's for his benefit, right?" Tegan said slowly.

"Yes," Renita said. "But you can never tell him. It's a big secret to keep. If you don't want to be part of this, now is the time to say so." *Just don't rat me out….*

Tegan got up and paced the room, stopped in front of the empty spot on the mantelpiece where the Brownlow Medal had sat. Absently, she dusted the gold-speckled marble with the heel of her hand.

Then she picked up a framed photo of her father in his football uniform, streaked with mud after a match. "He was happy when he was playing football," she said wistfully. "Ever since he bought the gym he's been up and down like a roller coaster, working all the time. The only way I see him is if I hang out in that cold, smelly place."

"If you want his gym to succeed then this is what it's going to take," Renita said.

Tegan dropped the photo on the marble ledge with a clatter. "Don't you get it? I don't *want* the gym to succeed. I want him to sell it and do something else.

He could be a coach or a phys ed teacher or some-thing. *Anything* else would take less time."

Renita blinked. She hadn't expected such ve-hemence from the girl. "Aren't you being a little selfish?"

"I'm not just thinking about me. He's totally stressed out. All he does is work. Work and worry."

Renita fell silent. There was an element of truth in that. Was she doing the right thing in trying to help Brett? Or would it be in his long-term interests to let his fitness center fail? Either way, did she have any right to affect his life so significantly? Especially when he'd turned down her offer to help?

She pressed her fingers to her temples. She didn't have answers. She only knew...

"He wants it," she said simply. "Whether you like it or not, the gym is important to him. I don't know why, but he needs to prove something to himself. I would like to give him the chance to do that."

Tegan stared at her. "Maybe that's what I don't get. You're basically giving him the money. How much is it costing?"

"One hundred and ninety thousand dollars. The price may go up if another buyer is interested. That's why I have to act quickly."

That in itself made her nervous. In fact, she was dizzy at the thought of spending this much money in one fell swoop. Usually when she made a major purchase like a car or her house, she researched the market, drew up a list of pros and cons, shopped around for weeks. Here, she'd made the decision to mortgage her life away in less than twenty-four hours.

Tegan threw herself back in her chair. "Why are you doing this?"

"He won't accept a loan." Renita began again with elaborate patience. She'd explained it already, in detail.

"No, I mean why are you *giving* him so much? Most women want to *get* money and presents from him. What are *you* getting out of it?"

Renita rose from the buttery leather couch, her arms folded as she crossed the room. She hadn't even asked herself that question.

Did she feel guilty that she hadn't given him the bank loan? Maybe a little. But not so guilty that she would go into debt for him. No, that wasn't why.

Did she hope that Brett would be so grateful he would love her, perhaps marry her? No. She could hope all she wanted for a lasting relationship with him. Giving him his medal back wouldn't guarantee that would happen. It could all blow up in her face if he found out.

Picking up the photo Tegan had been looking at, she saw it had been taken when Brett was in high school. As a teenager, he'd struggled to understand calculus and trigonometry. He'd worked so hard. With her help he'd been getting somewhere. He would have passed his final exam if she hadn't dropped his tutorials. In her own way, she'd hurt him every bit as much as he'd hurt her when he'd rejected her in front of his mates.

He was working hard at the gym, too. Busting his butt to make it happen, because he was too stubborn to figure out when to call it quits. Maybe this time he *would* succeed.

Renita glanced at Tegan. "Let's just say I owe him."

Tegan seemed surprised. Then, in her maddening teenage obstinacy, she asked, "Why?"

"You don't have to know everything," Renita said. "Do you want to help your father or not?"

She took a moment to think about that.

"I'll see what I can find out," she said finally and ran upstairs, her sock feet thudding on the carpeted steps.

Renita picked up her hair clip and put it in her purse. She wandered out of the living room and through the foyer. The dining room faced the driveway, and from here she could keep a lookout. It would be just their luck if Brett returned now.

In less than ten minutes Tegan was thundering down the stairs again. "Is this it?" she said excitedly, handing Renita a business card. "I found it in his jacket pocket. Simon J. Toltz, Dealer in Antiquities, Fine Jewelry and Memorabilia."

"That's got to be it!" Renita copied down the phone number and address and tucked her notepad in her purse. "Put that back where you found it. I'll go home and call this man." Impulsively, she gave Tegan a hug. "Thank you. You did great."

Tegan's smile was hesitant, but her cheeks were pink. "Promise you'll tell me what happens?"

Renita nodded. "I promise."

BRETT SAT AT HIS DESK, adding up the sum total of his net worth—not counting what was under dispute in the courts. He could probably get thirty thousand for his E320 Mercedes, but then he'd have to buy another car, and with the price of automobiles these days he wouldn't be able to get anything decent below ten thousand. That left him twenty. His Rolex was worth a few thousand. He could probably get something for his Collingwood team jersey....

He tossed the pen down and leaned back, rubbing the heels of his hands over his eyes. What the hell had he come to, giving his life away in a fire sale?

He picked up the pen and tapped it on his cheek. What else did he have worth selling?

The house.

His heart sank at the thought of telling Tegan they had to move. She loved this place, the nearby beach, the sailing club. It had been the consolation prize for taking her away from her mother, her old school and her friends.

On the other hand, how could he ever face Renita again if he didn't get himself out of this mess?

The phone rang. Slowly, he picked it up. "Hello?"

"Brett? Simon Toltz here. We have a new bidder…."

GRASPING A FIVE-POUND dumbbell in each hand, Renita did a biceps curl before pushing them up over her head. Perspiration trickled down her temples. She couldn't wait for the gym to reopen.

Her phone lay on her coffee table, which was pushed back against the couch so she had some space to maneuver in her living room. She expected Brett to ring at any time with the news. She would have to act surprised. Then pleased—

The doorbell rang.

Startled, Renita peered through the sheers and saw Brett's car in the driveway. He was *here*. And she was wearing her blue sports bra, the one she never wore in public, and a pair of black running shorts. She'd expected him to phone first.

The doorbell rang again.

Oh, God. She didn't want him to see her in this top.

She grabbed a trench coat from the hall closet, then opened the door. Brett's grin stretched wide above a huge bouquet of red roses.

"Hey, Brett." Seeing him so happy was worth every penny she'd spent on the medal. She stepped back to let him in.

"These are for you," he said, offering her the flowers.

"Thank you." She buried her nose in the fragrant blooms. "It's a little early for Valentine's Day."

"I've got good news." He glanced from the furniture pushed against the walls to the exercise mat and the set of hand weights. "It's great that you're keeping up your training program." He took in her coat and bare legs. "But in a trench coat?"

"I know I look ridiculous." Not to mention she was boiling. "It's this top I'm wearing."

"Let me see." He reached for her.

She edged away. "I'll put these in water." She headed for the kitchen. *Red* roses. Keeping her voice carefully casual, she said over her shoulder, "What's your good news?"

"I sold my Brownlow Medal. This time it's a done deal. The money was transferred to my account last night via online banking."

Renita put the sheaf of flowers on the kitchen counter. Hearing his joy, she didn't have to fake her excitement. "Oh, Brett, that's wonderful! What a relief."

"I wasn't worried. *Much*." Grinning, he enveloped her in a bear hug and lifted her off the ground. With his face buried in her damp ponytail, he said in a muffled voice, "Sorry I was such a pig the last time you saw me."

"You *were* a pig." Kissing him, she slid back to the floor. When she eased back, all warm and disheveled, her coat flopped open.

Before she could pull it closed, Brett was tugging

it off her shoulders. "Don't be silly. You're going to overheat."

Her arms snaked protectively around her bare midriff.

"Surely you're not still self-conscious about your body. I've seen you naked."

"That's different. In this sports bra and shorts my gut billows out like the Pillsbury Doughboy."

Gently but firmly he pulled her arms away to see for himself. "You exaggerate—you know that, don't you? You're beautiful and sexy."

Renita ducked away. She wanted to believe him. He'd convinced her the night they'd made love. Why hadn't that stuck? She reached into the cabinet under the sink for a tall crystal vase. Keeping her body angled away from him, she filled it with water, then unwrapped the tissue from the flowers and started clipping the ends off the stems with kitchen scissors. "Let me have a shower, then we can celebrate."

"Or I could shower with you." With a fingertip he stroked away tiny beads of perspiration in the hollow of her spine.

She shivered at his delicious touch as she tucked the last rose in the vase. "Do you think you can snap at me and then charm your way back into my arms?"

"I don't know. Can I?" He brushed his lips over her shoulder. Then he turned her and bent his head to kiss her again, overriding her reluctance with a gentle assault on her mouth, teasing her lips open as he lifted her arms around his neck.

For a moment Renita surrendered to his kiss. Then she eased back.

Brett groaned. "Now what?"

"Who bought your Brownlow?" She had to be sure that Simon Toltz hadn't spilled the beans.

Brett's hands stilled on her arms. "I don't know. The buyer wanted to be anonymous. I'm happy, but I can't believe it's really gone this time."

Relieved, Renita stroked the muscles at the base of his neck. "You'll get your Brownlow Medal back someday."

"You don't know these collectors. Once they get hold of a coveted object, they never sell it. It might turn up in a deceased estate years from now. Or not."

"No, you will. I feel sure of it."

"I appreciate the sentiment. And I appreciate your offer of a personal loan, even if I couldn't accept it."

"I—" Renita broke off, not sure what she could say.

"Look at the strife we've already had over your bank holding my business loan. Can you imagine the problems if I owed you that much money, personally?"

Her throat dried up. A shaky laugh rasped out. "I guess it's lucky you didn't accept."

"Oh, baby, you'd better believe it." Kissing her, he

pulled her sports bra over her head, then cupped her small breasts in his palms.

"They're not very big," she whispered.

"They're just right. Perfect." He bent his head and sucked one hard bud into his mouth, eliciting a soft moan from deep in her throat.

Though she'd never made love in a kitchen full of warm afternoon sun, Renita gave in to the spirit of the moment. Her shorts and underpants slipped down her hips, tangled at her feet before she kicked them away. She refused to look at the red lines where the shorts elastic had cut into her flesh. Brett didn't seem to care or notice as he lifted her onto the counter. He nudged apart her legs and pressed his fingers into her dark curls.

Suddenly he took her hard, holding her gaze as he moved inside her.

Renita clung to his sweat-drenched shoulders, riding a wave that peaked and crashed and built again until she was mindless and boneless, saturated with pleasure.

BRETT OPENED HIS EYES and eased his arm out from under Renita's head. She slept on, her breathing deep and slow.

Shadows stretched across her bedroom floor. Through the half-drawn curtains, the sun was low in the sky. After they'd made love in the kitchen, they'd moved to a more comfortable setting to do it again. And again.

Leaning over now, he checked her bedside clock.

Seven o'clock. They'd slept for a couple of hours. After the strain of the past weeks he could hardly believe that stress was over. Now he felt rejuvenated. He could begin to forge ahead with his business plans.

And with his relationship with Renita. He studied her face as she lay sleeping. She had a quiet beauty. Yes, she was still overweight, but she was getting fit, and that was important to him. He smiled, thinking of her hiding in a trench coat. She'd get over that in time. He'd help her do that, too.

He touched her shoulder. She opened her eyes, looking straight into his. He curled his fingers around the back of her neck as he pressed a lingering kiss on her lips. "Sorry to wake you, but it's getting late," he said, easing back. "Tegan will be wondering where I am."

Renita stretched, twisting languorously beneath the sheets. "I need to get up, too, and feed the animals. I'm surprised Lucy hasn't barged in here already, demanding her kibble."

Brett leaned over the side of the bed, grabbed his jeans and found his phone. "Hey, Tegan," he said when she picked up. "Everything okay, sweetheart? I'm at Renita's. We lost track of the time." He winked at Renita. "Will do. I'll be home soon."

He hung up and slipped the phone back in his pocket. "She said to say hi to you. Funny, I thought for a while she was a little jealous of you."

"Um, no, I think we're good now. Must be because

I introduced her to Oliver," Renita said. "Give her my best."

"Do you want to go out for dinner tomorrow night?" Brett pulled on his jeans. "It'll be just us. Tegan's going to stay with Amber for the weekend."

Renita got up and slipped on a dressing gown. "Poppy, my assistant, is having a birthday party at the pub tomorrow. Do you want to do that instead?"

"Sure." He pulled her into his embrace for another kiss. "Everything's turning out great."

"Yes," she said, oddly subdued. Going to the dresser, she began brushing her hair in front of the mirror.

Brett watched her for a moment, puzzled, then shrugged and picked up his shirt. As he dressed, he examined the wall unit, which was cluttered with tattered hardback books, obviously treasured copies, plus a decorative box of some sort and a collection of African hair ornaments. And on the end of the shelf…Pluto? Brett picked up the yellow plastic toy and pressed the button that made the legs collapse.

"Is this the one I gave you? I'd forgotten all about it." Pluto, her favorite cartoon character, because she loved dogs.

"I guess you think it's weird that I kept it, huh?" Renita was watching him in the mirror.

"It's nice." His voice sounded odd and he cleared his throat. "I've given women diamond necklaces they've seemed to care less about."

He met her gaze. Again, he was puzzled by her expression. She looked sad or something. Thoughtfully, he replaced the toy. "Is everything all right?"

"Fine." Renita tugged on a strand of her hair. "How would I look as a blonde?"

"Not like the Renita I know."

"That might be a good thing."

"Don't be silly." He sat on the bed to put on his socks. "I could take Tegan in early and we could see a movie before the party."

"Can't. I'm going shopping."

"Again? You went just last week." The words slipped out before he could stop them. He'd been sensitized by Amber's habits of overconsumption. "Forget it, it's none of my business."

"I need things. Underwear and stuff."

"Oh, I get it—because you've lost weight. I noticed from your chart you've lost six inches."

She spun around. "You read my chart?"

"Hey!" He winced. "It's my job to keep track of clients' progress."

"Tegan said you never looked at the charts."

Brett snorted. "She doesn't know *everything,* much as she likes to think she does."

Renita's cheeks were bright red. Hell, did she think he cared that she'd lost two of those inches off her bust? Although if she'd been just any client he probably would have praised her for the loss. She was sensitive about her body image. Her being a client made everything trickier.

"When Tegan and I were in Chadstone I found a private medical clinic where they do cosmetic surgery," Renita said.

"Oh, yeah?" Why was she telling him this?

She took a brochure off the dresser and handed it to him. "I've been thinking about cosmetic surgery for a while. I went back to the mall last week and had a consultation with the surgeon. He explained the options, the potential side effects. I had to do a psychological assessment, but then I signed the papers and paid a deposit. It's all booked."

"*What* is booked?"

"Breast implants."

He stared, vaguely aware that his jaw had dropped. "Do I have hearing problems or have you gone insane?"

Hurt flashed in her eyes. Then she lifted her chin. "What's wrong with implants?"

He flipped his palms up. "I don't know where to begin. You have perfectly lovely breasts."

"You're just saying that to make me feel good. Amber's are huge. That's the woman you *married*."

"Not for her br—" He broke off. He'd been barely twenty, green as the turf he played on, his head turned by sudden fame and too much money. Influenced by his mates and surrounded by football groupies who were all some variation of Amber. Brett was ashamed to admit it, but back then the size of a girl's breasts *had* factored into his choice of girlfriend.

"Ah." Renita read his hesitation correctly.

"That was *then*. I divorced Amber, remember? Her breasts certainly weren't enough to keep us together." He shook his head. "I can't believe I'm having this conversation. Isn't a guy allowed to grow up?"

"I'm not doing this for you," Renita said. "It's for me, to feel better about myself."

"What's wrong with simply being healthy and fit?"

"Nothing. But since I've lost weight my breasts have gotten smaller. They're not in proportion to my hips."

"You look fine. What is this obsession with being perfect? You're beautiful and sexy just as you are."

"The surgery is already booked. I've paid a deposit." Her voice was firm.

"It's up to you, of course. It's your body." Brett exhaled forcefully. He didn't understand how she could be so strong in some ways, and yet so vulnerable. Had he somehow contributed to her insecurity?

She'd turned back to the mirror to study herself, a tiny frown drawing her eyebrows together. Taking hold of her shoulders, he kissed the back of her neck. "You look fabulous. I'll see you tomorrow night."

Meeting his gaze in the mirror, she smiled. But the crease between her brows was still there.

CHAPTER THIRTEEN

"THE ROPE GOES THROUGH the loop, around and back through, then pull tight," Brett explained to Tegan, above the sounds of shrieking kids splashing in the shallows.

They were seated on the steps of one of the beach huts at Summerside Beach, practicing knots before Tegan's sailing lesson. That is, they were trying to. Brett's cell phone rang for the umpteenth time.

Tegan groaned. "So much for quality time."

Brett took the call from Janet—they had more to discuss about the grand opening two weeks from today. He should be at the gym, but he'd barely seen Tegan all week.

Brett hung up. "Sorry about that. Now where were we?"

"I've got the bowline figured out." She tossed down her ropes and stretched her bare legs, wriggling her toes in the sand. "Dad?"

"Hmm?" He brushed away a persistent fly and squinted at the diagram, the lines of which seemed to dance in the bright sunlight. It was hard to concentrate when he was thinking about membership deals and trial classes of Zumba and—

"Are we broke?"

Brett glanced up sharply. "Where'd you get that idea?"

"I'm not dumb, Dad, and I'm not a little kid anymore. I know it must cost a lot of money to buy a business and all that equipment."

"I have a bank loan," he reminded her.

"But you had to sell your Brownlow Medal."

A boy ran past, kicking up sand. Brett hesitated. "I've paid for the equipment. Everything's fine now."

Tegan's eyes, shaded beneath her billed cap, were huge. "You should have told me before you did it."

"I…was ashamed," he admitted, then had to look away. The admission was gut-wrenching.

"I don't mind being poor."

"We're not poor!" He spoke more harshly than he intended.

She was quiet for a moment. "We could get a smaller house, farther from the beach."

"What about the sailing club?"

She sighed. "Dad, I don't *like* sailing."

He blinked. "This is the first I've heard of it."

"That's because you don't listen! I never wanted to join the sailing club. *You* wanted me to." She was on her feet now, tugging down her shorts, digging her toes in the sand.

"I thought you were enjoying it." Or had he wanted

her to enjoy experiences he'd never had? He took a deep breath. "I'm listening now. What *do* you want to do?"

"Dance. I'd like to take lessons in modern dance."

"Dance." Brett tossed down the lengths of rope, pointless now.

Tegan leaned down and put her arms around his neck. She smelled of salt and sand. "Are you happy, Daddy? Was it worth it, selling your Brownlow Medal? Is the gym worth it?"

"It was worth it." He squeezed her hand and rested his cheek against her sun-warmed forearm. "The Brownlow is only a piece of metal, in the end."

If he kept telling himself that, one day he would believe it.

"Someday you can buy it back."

Odd. Renita had said the same thing. He twisted his head to look at his daughter's face. "I couldn't even if I had the money. I don't know who bought it."

"Oh. Right." Tegan pulled away from him and walked across the beach to the water, rubbing her arms as if she was cold, even though it was a sizzling hot day.

"Tegan?" Brett watched her wade into the water and stand there up to her knees, looking out across the bay. Teenagers were so moody….

The soles of his bare feet burned as he hopped across the hot sand to step gratefully into the cool water. Wrapping his arm around Tegan's shoulders, he hugged her tightly to his side. A tear wove a silver streak down her sun-pinked cheek. "What's wrong?"

"Maybe I should live with Mum," she said with a hiccup. "Then you'd have more time to put into the gym. I know how important it is to you."

Hell. Where had this come from? "*You're* important to me." He wiped away the tear with the pad of his thumb. "No more talk like that, you hear? I want you with me."

She shrugged and sniffed, as if not quite convinced. Then she glanced down the beach toward the sailing club, where other teens were gathering to carry their dinghies into the water. "Do I have to take the sailing lesson? You could drive me into the city early."

"That would leave Amy without a partner. Let's stick to the original plan. After your lesson we'll tell the instructor you won't be back." He gave her another hug and then a nudge. "Try not to crash the boat your last time out."

She gave him a wan smile and ran off.

Brett left the beach and headed for the gym. He put in an hour sweating over the books, then flipped through the newspaper, scanning the columns for a mention of the sale of his Brownlow Medal. Renita and Tegan had put the idea into his head that someday he might be able to buy it back. He could only do that if he knew who'd bought it. Simon Toltz had promised to be discreet, but Brett understood how these things worked. When something big happened in the sports world there was always a leak to the media.

Aha! On page six a brief article reported the anonymous purchase of Brett O'Connor's Brownlow Medal for nearly two hundred thousand dollars. That was it. No names.

"Anything interesting?" Janet asked, looking over his shoulder.

Brett started to fold the newspaper, then realized it was pointless. He stabbed a finger at the two-inch column. "I might as well tell you, since reporters will probably call the gym. I had to sell my Brownlow Medal to pay for the refurbishment."

"No way." Her eyes widened as she searched his face and realized he was serious. "I thought you had a bank loan."

"It didn't cover everything."

"Brett, that's terrible." Janet squeezed his forearm. "I'm so sorry."

"Hey, no biggie." He forced a smile. "The good news is it paid for the new equipment." It felt satisfying to say that. He was a man again, in control of his life, not beholden to anyone.

"I appreciate your support," he went on. "I felt like a jerk asking you and Mark to wait for your paychecks. The money from the sale of my medal went into my account yesterday afternoon, and I immediately transferred your pay. It'll be available as of this morning."

"You think?" Janet cocked her head skeptically. "With the speed of computers it *should* be instantaneous. But it takes the bank three days to process any transaction."

"You should switch to the Community Bank," Brett said. "I've never had such great service."

"I *am* with the Community Bank. *Instantly?*" She huffed out a laugh. "I forgot you have connections. Renita must have pulled strings for you."

"No," he said. "Renita doesn't pull strings for anyone. She goes strictly by the book."

Janet frowned. "When did you make the sale?"

"Thursday evening."

"And the money was in your account Friday morning? I think you'll find she's had a hand in this."

Brett frowned. Maybe Renita had relaxed her principles for him. But the more he thought about it, the more it struck him that something bigger might be going on. It was strange that she'd been so certain he'd get his medal back one day. Why would she think that unless she had a role in the transaction?

Maybe she even knew who the buyer was.

BRETT PARKED BEHIND the pub. Driving Tegan to Amber's apartment in the city had taken longer than he'd expected. Glancing at his watch, he saw he'd probably missed dinner.

He locked his car and walked around to the pub entrance. The heat of the day had given way to a balmy evening. Savory smells from the restaurants dotting the shopping strip mingled with the tang of the citronella tree that shaded the village square.

A buzzing party atmosphere spilled out of the open doors. Above the voices, laughter and the tinkling of glasses, he could hear music. Karaoke was in full swing in the private room at the back. A woman was singing, badly off-key.

Brett ordered a draft beer at the bar. Sipping through the foam, he picked his way across the lounge to the function room. In the low lighting, three long tables were crowded with partygoers. Dinner *was* over, judging by the empty plates, but the drinks were still flowing.

Renita was the singer on the dais, holding a microphone up to her red-lipsticked mouth. She wore a short black dress with a plunging neckline. With her head thrown back, she belted out a song about needing a hero. Her voice cracked on the high notes, but what she lacked in musicality she made up for in enthusiasm.

He had to chuckle at seeing yet another side to her. She was still his buddy, his pal. Yet now Renita was hot, even if she still didn't know it. No, she wasn't his "type." That's what he loved about her.

The song ended to a drunken roar of applause from the tables in front. A blond woman in a V-necked top and black pants climbed up eagerly to take the microphone. Renita, tottering slightly in four-inch heels, stepped off the platform with elaborate care, arms raised for balance. Safely on the floor, she flung back her hair with a triumphant smile.

Brett started forward, hand raised to catch her attention. Before he could make eye contact, a slick young dude in a sports jacket guided her to an empty chair…beside his. One hand held hers and his other hand was on her waist.

No, now his hand was on her butt. Brett's smile flattened. He lengthened his stride to rescue Renita from this groping lounge lizard, but he nearly stumbled when she leaned in flirtatiously, all but batting her eyelids at the guy. The creep murmured in her ear. Renita laughed and rested her hand on his forearm.

Brett came to a halt, trying to figure out what was going on here. Renita wasn't the type to flaunt her body, yet that's exactly what she was doing.

Thanks to Amber, he was all too familiar with the body language of a woman on the prowl. Renita was preening, touching her hair, pushing her arms together and leaning on the table to emphasize her cleavage.

She was also drunk. When she raised her glass she nearly missed her mouth, then giggled when a few drops of sparkling wine fizzed down her chin. No wonder she was acting this way. She didn't know what she was doing.

Her admirer immediately topped up her glass from a bottle on the table. Clearly, he expected the evening to end with Renita in his bed.

Brett carefully set his beer on a nearby table.
Not bloody likely, mate.

RENITA GUZZLED BACK her champagne, feeling
pleased with herself. Lexie complained that she
couldn't sing. What the hell did she know?

"No touching my butt," she said to Craig, wagging
a finger at him.

Craig was an idiot, but he was a distraction from
the sense of doom that was driving her, literally, to
drink. Brett should be here any minute. She couldn't
wait to see him, but she was also dreading it. His
happiness and relief at his financial crisis being over
was wonderful. But the stress of keeping such a huge
secret from him—and having so many other people
in on the secret—was taking its toll on her.

Someone squeezed her shoulder. For a moment she
was confused, because both Craig's hands were on
the table. Then she saw another hand clamp Craig's
shoulder. She squinted at the long fingers and the
gold hair on the wrist. Hey, that hand was familiar.

"Brett!" She swiveled in her chair, delight over-
coming the dread at seeing him. "I didn't know you
were here."

"Clearly." He turned to Craig. "I'm Brett, Renita's
date."

Craig took one look at the tall, broad-shouldered
athlete and got the hint. "Hey, Julie," he said to the
redheaded woman on his right, "how's it going in
Payroll?"

"Let's get out of here," Brett said to Renita. "There's something I want to ask you about."

Renita wasn't ready to be alone with him. "I'm having a good time." She drained the last drops from her glass, then shook the champagne bottle. It was empty. Looking around for the waiter, she met Brett's exasperated stare. "What's *your* problem?"

He dropped to a crouch next to her. "You've drunk a lot," he said, so quietly she had to strain to hear over the music and conversation. "I want us to leave."

Concentrating really hard on listening, Renita heard him say "us." *She and Brett were an "us."* People who were linked like that didn't keep secrets.

"I'm not drunk," she said, waving her glass. "I never drink more than two glasses of wine." She frowned. "Although s'hard to count when the glass is never empty. Imagine that! A wineglass that never empties. They should put that on the market. It'd make a fortune. Don't you think, Brett? Huh?"

"Please come with me, Renita."

When he asked her like that, looking straight into her eyes, it was impossible to say no.

Standing unsteadily, she grabbed her purse. "Bye, everyone. I'm going." She waved to her assistant at the head of the table. "Happy Birthday, Poppy."

A chorus of protests rose from the group. "You can't go," Poppy said. "We haven't had the cake yet!"

Brett tugged on her arm, urging her away from

the table. She went, but the closer she got to the exit the more worried she became. Dumb idea, getting drunk. She would end up blurting everything out.

She dragged her feet. "I don't want to leave."

"Craig is a creep," Brett said.

"He's not that bad," she replied automatically. It was easier to pick a fight with Brett than to tell him what she'd done.

"He had his hands all over you."

"You're jealous."

"No, I'm not."

"Yes, you are. You can't handle that other men find me attractive. You want to hold me back."

"I don't want to hold you back. I'm having enough trouble holding you up," he said, adjusting his grip around her waist. "Is that what you want—to go out with other men?"

"No, but…"

"But it's okay to flirt and let them grope you when I'm not around."

"Don't you trust me?"

"Should I?"

"Course you should," she said, swaying on her feet. She struggled to focus on his face. "*I love you.* I want you to know that, if…when…"

"Renita, you're pissed as a newt," he said. "Please come away from here."

She might have gone quietly then, but their exit was prevented by the arrival of a three-layer cake with chocolate icing, sizzling with sparklers. It was so big it had to be carried by two people.

Mmm, cake. She followed the procession with her eyes.

Brett reached for her hand. "You don't want that."

Before she'd come out tonight she'd told herself she wasn't going to taste a single morsel of delicious, fattening cake. Then she'd gone and used up practically a week's worth of calories on wine. So what the hell, she might as well eat cake, too.

"I may be in love with you," she said, untangling her hand from his grasp. "But that doesn't mean you can tell me what to eat."

"I didn't mean it like that," Brett said. "But you'll be sick if you put a load of sugar on top of alcohol."

He might be right, but she felt compelled to take a stand. She was no doormat. *She* decided when she was going home. *And* if she was going to gorge herself on cake. If he didn't like it, too bad.

"I have changed my mind," she announced carefully and with immense dignity. "I am returning to the party."

Brett put his hands up in surrender. "Fine. Enjoy yourself. I'll wait in the bar. When you're ready, I'll drive you home."

Was he making sure she didn't go home with Craig? "You don't have to do that. We've got a party bus and a chauffeur. No one's driving."

"I'm glad to hear it. Then all I have to say is, keep away from Craig."

"I'll talk to whoever I please. *Whom*ever."

"You do that." Shaking his head, he turned and walked out.

She watched him go. Her vision was a little blurry, but even so, she was certain she could see the thread of their relationship unraveling.

A JACKHAMMER WAS DRILLING into Renita's brain. Her mouth was stuffed with cotton wool. She opened her eyes and was blinded by a flash of sunlight coming through the window. She'd forgotten to draw the curtains.

But her memory of the night before was more painful than even this mother of all hangovers. Unable to move without hurting, she lay as still as possible and counted her regrets.

Number one: drinking too much champagne. Wa-a-ay too much.

Number two: eating an enormous piece of chocolate fudge cake with chocolate cream cheese frosting.

Number three: not talking things out with Brett and coming clean about the Brownlow Medal. She couldn't take this level of stress any longer.

Number four: the second piece of cake.

Number five: telling Brett she loved him. Was she an idiot? It was too soon!

Groaning, she rolled onto her stomach and pulled the pillow over her head.

Regret number six: refusing to leave with him. If she'd gone home when he'd first asked, she'd have no list of regrets.

Well, except for drinking too much. And there was no guarantee that in her state last night she would have had the guts to confess.

Lucy put her yellow paws on the mattress and licked Renita's arm.

"Hey, Luce," Renita mumbled. At least her dog would always love her, no matter how much of an idiot she was.

Throwing back the covers, she dragged herself out of bed and into a scalding shower. Breakfast was coffee, toast, bacon and eggs. That was the other problem with a hangover; the antidote was copious amounts of greasy food.

Feeling slightly better, she padded out to the backyard to feed Frankie.

The cockatoo tilted his head and stared at her through one round, yellow-rimmed eye. "You're a poop."

"Yeah, I know." She stroked the bird's white feathers. "I can't live like this, Frankie. I have to tell him. Even if he hates me."

She went back inside and, in an attempt to lift her spirits, changed into a summery skirt and blouse. She did her hair and makeup, dotting concealer on the dark circles under her eyes.

Her stomach was churning again as she rang Brett's doorbell, whether from the bacon or the coming confrontation, she wasn't sure. She'd acted out of the goodness of her heart; surely he would see that.

Brett opened the door, his mouth twisted in an ironic smile. "How are we feeling this morning? A tad hungover, perhaps?"

"Not too flash. But it's big of you to revel in my pain. Um, can I come in?"

"Are you sure you want to? You didn't seem to care for my company last night."

"I'd like to apologize."

He stepped back to let her in. The house seemed unnaturally quiet with Tegan away. He led through the formal dining room into the kitchen. "I was finishing breakfast. Want anything?"

"Just coffee, thanks. I'm afraid to add any more food to the mix." She pulled out a wicker chair opposite his place at the breakfast table. The sunny nook looked onto a garden of flowering shrubs and gravel paths. The remains of a boiled egg sat next to his bowl of fruit and yogurt.

Brett brought her a cup of coffee. He picked up his spoon and dug into the strawberries and yogurt. "Go ahead. Grovel away."

"You could at least look at me."

He glanced up. "Well?"

Immediately she dropped her gaze. "I'm sorry.

I know you were just trying to help me last night."
See? Wanting to help is a good motive.

Brett nodded and went on eating.

"Craig *is* a creep. Even when I'm drunk, I'm aware of that." She was stalling. She had to get to the point before she completely lost her nerve. Honesty was proving to be more painful than a champagne headache.

Brett's gaze sharpened. "Did he give you trouble after I left?"

"Not at all. He turned his attentions elsewhere."

Brett set his bowl aside. "Why did you flirt with him? Is there something you need that I'm not giving you?"

"No." She picked up her cup, then set it down again. She wished he wouldn't be so nice. It made this harder.

"Did you mean what you said?" He reached for her hand and turned it over, thoughtfully tracing the life line with his fingertip. "About loving me?"

"I didn't want to fall in love with you," she said. "When you first came back to Summerside I didn't want anything to do with you."

"You made that pretty clear." He met her gaze. "Things have changed, though. You've changed. I've changed. I never thought I'd get together with some-one so quickly after splitting with Amber, but you're different. I should have been with a woman like you from the beginning." Curling her fingers into her palm, he brought her hand to his lips. "I love you, too."

They were words she'd longed to hear. Now they only made her feel guiltier.

"Brett." Renita squeezed her eyes shut, tears seeping out at the corners. "There's something I have to tell you about your Brownlow."

CHAPTER FOURTEEN

"I WAS HOPING YOU WOULD say something about my Brownlow Medal," Brett said, pushing his breakfast dishes aside. "I was going to ask you last night, but you were too drunk, and frankly, too belligerent. It was like you were trying to pick a fight with me so we didn't have to talk."

She opened her eyes. If he was disappointed she hadn't responded to his declaration, it was clear he wasn't going to express it. There were too many issues for them to talk of love, anyway.

"Just because I'm not great with numbers doesn't mean I'm stupid." Brett leaned forward. "You know who bought it, don't you?"

She swallowed. But when she opened her mouth to speak she couldn't seem to get the words out. Finally she croaked, "Yes."

"I knew it! You were so sure that I would get it back someday. You were very insistent."

"I was, wasn't I?" she said dismally.

"Then there's how fast the money was transferred between accounts. That could only happen with behind-the-scenes help at the bank. *Your* help."

Her silence must have seemed to confirm his suspicion.

"I'm positive you know the buyer. Maybe you even orchestrated the deal. You obviously trust him, because you bypassed protocol to process the transaction quickly."

She fiddled with the leather strap of her watch, avoiding his gaze.

"Well?" he said. "Is that what happened?"

"Er, something like that." She pulled her untouched coffee toward her. The steam had stopped rising.

Brett sucked in a deep breath. "I'm trying not to be angry that you went behind my back—"

She made a strangled sound, started to speak.

"Hear me out," Brett said. "You were attempting to help so I'm not going to go ballistic, even though you were aware I don't want to be beholden to you."

Renita's hands curled in on themselves.

"But you've got to tell me." Brett leaned forward. "Who bought my Brownlow Medal?"

The silence stretched, magnifying the ticking of the wall clock. Finally, she whispered, "I did."

Brett froze. The blood drained from his cheeks. "You!"

"You can have it back anytime," she said in a rush. "I don't want it for myself. I only bought it so you wouldn't lose it forever to an unknown collector."

"You paid nearly two hundred thousand dollars

for something you don't want and have no use for?"
He slumped back in his chair, shaking his head in
disbelief. "Where did you get that kind of money?"

"I took out a second mortgage," she said, hunch-
ing down in her chair. Her head was pounding worse
than ever. "I was certain you'd buy it back from me
when you could."

"It's just another way of giving me a personal
loan." He paused before saying, "You *knew* how I
felt about this. Going ahead and buying my medal
showed zero respect for my wishes. I would rather a
stranger had bought it. Then at least I'd be free and
clear of debt."

Color flooded back into Renita's cheeks. "I thought
since we were a couple it made sense. I thought you'd
be pleased. Grateful, even. Guess I thought wrong."

"You were my buddy, Renita. The woman I laughed
with, made love to. Fell in love with. And now—
now you *own* me."

"Not just me," she said miserably. "Jack has a
stake. And so do…your parents."

He stared at her. "You went to my *parents* for
money to bail me out?"

"Only five thousand. I'm going to repay them
first. I should be able to get it to them within thirty
days."

"They can't afford it, not even for a month!"

Anger shimmered in the air between them. They'd
fought before and made up. Renita knew with a dull,

sick certainty that they weren't going to bounce back from this.

"Did you even stop to think what this would mean for our relationship? For my life?" he demanded.

"I—" Renita faltered. She'd only considered two things. Saving the gym and saving the medal. Wasn't that enough?

"If I want to take Tegan on a trip, first I have to consider what I owe you." Brett pushed away from the table to pace across the tiled floor. He spun back. "If I want to buy you a present I will only have the money because *you* made it possible. What if we break up? You'd resent me, if not despise me, over a sacrifice you made for nothing. This will hang over my head every second of every day until I can pay you back."

"There's no hurry," she said in a small voice.

He began to pace again, gesturing angrily. "Plus I'll have your sacrifice on my conscience. What if you need money for something?"

"I know you'll discharge the debt as soon as you can," she rallied to argue. Anyone would think she'd tried to hurt him, the way he was carrying on. "Your money will be freed up when your divorce is settled. You told me it was only a matter of time."

"*If* Amber agrees to my terms. That's not certain, by any means. And I may only get a fraction of what I expect."

Renita tilted her head to one side. "So were you

lying before when you asked the bank for a second loan?"

He stopped moving abruptly, clearly aware of his tactical error. "I was being optimistic."

"You're supposed to be accurate. But that was never your strong point, was it?" She rose abruptly, scraping her chair over the tiles. She smoothed down her skirt. "If this is going to cause problems between us, you can have the medal. My gift to you."

"Don't be ridiculous. I can't accept a gift of two hundred thousand dollars."

"If we're *friends,* if you love me, it's not ridiculous." She paused, then added quietly, "Or was that a lie, too?"

He flinched. "No! But how can we be friends, or lovers…or even equals, if you're always wondering whether I'm with you because I owe you?"

"You mean, if you feel less of a man," she said flatly.

"You're no one to talk about insecurities. With this much money between us, how will either of us ever know for sure what's true and real?" He slid onto a barstool at the kitchen counter and dropped his head in his hands. "Renita, Renita, what have you done?"

"I was only trying to—"

"Help," he said bitterly. "Yeah, I get it. It was an incredibly generous thing to do. And a terrible mistake."

"I wouldn't have had to save you if you'd listened to me in the first place."

"You wouldn't have had to 'save' me if you'd shown confidence in me." He got to his feet, his expression stony. "I think you'd better go."

She started to panic. "We're not going to talk this out?"

"What is there to talk about?"

"Our future?"

He pushed the stool roughly up to the counter. "Keep the damn medal. Sell it and get your money back. I don't care about it anymore."

"You. Don't. Care." Renita slowly went to pick up the purse she'd dropped in his front hall. Her voice was quiet, halting, when she said, "How dare you say that after what I sacrificed to get it."

"You see? You're already throwing it in my face."

She slammed the door shut behind her.

THE PARKING LOT was jammed with cars when Renita arrived at the gym a week later. She hadn't been for any training sessions and she'd forgotten today was the grand opening. She parked on the side of the road a block away and walked back along the leafy sidewalk. Brett O'Connor Fitness Center read the sign above the door. Streamers and balloons decorated the entryway pillars.

She ran into her father in the parking lot next to

the barbecue set up for a sausage sizzle. He held a sausage wrapped in bread in one hand and a soft drink in the other.

"Where's your gym gear? Brett's running nonstop classes and a marathon bike ride—"

"I'm not here to exercise. In fact, I won't be coming to the gym for a while. It's awkward. Brett and I… we had a thing going on." It was impossible to keep her voice steady. "But we broke up."

"Oh, Renita. I was afraid something like this would happen," Steve grumbled. "You're better off without him."

She *so* didn't want to talk about this right now. "Dad, I've got to go. I'm just dropping something off for Brett."

"What about the Fun Run in a couple of weeks? You're still going to do that, aren't you? We've hardly had a chance to train together. I was hoping we could step that up between now and the run."

Oh, hell. How could she have forgotten the Fun Run? Her breast surgery was scheduled for next Saturday. The day of the run she would still be recovering. She couldn't bounce the girls and risk tearing out the stitches. It made her wince just to think of it. "We'll have to see." She felt bad about lying to her dad but she knew what he'd think about implants and she wasn't in the mood.

Renita hadn't picked the best day for her mission. Tightening her grip on her shoulder bag with her precious cargo, she stepped into the gym, nonetheless.

A whiteboard at reception detailed the schedule of classes and special events. Brett and his team had worked toward this for months and it was finally happening. The refurbishment was complete. The entire gym, including the new equipment, gleamed.

She edged her way through the milling crowd. More streamers and balloons decorated the refreshment area. There were probably well over a hundred people here—regulars and guests. Thumping feet overhead attested to a group fitness class happening upstairs. The cardio room was packed. Janet was conducting a spin class; Matt was demonstrating the weight machines.

Brett had taken over a squash court to lead a group in a Boxercise. He wore a sleeveless tank top. Greedily, she took in his glistening shoulders and fierce concentration as he fielded punches with a padded shield. The teenage boy throwing them appeared set to prove he could be the next featherweight champ.

Next to her, a sweat-drenched woman with a towel slung around her neck was talking excitedly on her cell phone. "You've got to get down here. Memberships are half price today only. No, the gym's not like that anymore. You wouldn't believe how this place has improved."

"Hey, Renita!" Tegan was circulating with a tray of Dixie cups. "Do you want a Powerade?"

"No, thanks…. This is amazing."

"We've signed up so many new members I've lost count." Tegan paused. "How come you told him?"

"I'm not good at keeping secrets. He guessed, anyway."

"I think it sucks that you and Dad stopped seeing each other."

"Do you mean that?" Renita asked warily.

"I know I wasn't that nice to you. But you're actually kind of cool. At least, you don't act phony with me."

"Thanks." Renita smiled, touched by the girl's admission. "I need to talk to Brett. When will he be finished with Boxercise?"

Tegan checked the clock above the shiny new cappuccino machine. "In a few minutes."

Renita saw Brett glance her way through the glass wall of the squash court. She waved. The teenage boy landed a punch that sent Brett staggering. *Oops.* She'd broken his concentration.

"I'll wait over here," Renita mouthed.

The cappuccino machine was self-serve. She put a mug under the spigot, slotted in a dollar and pressed a button.

"It's excellent coffee," a woman in yoga gear enthused, mug in hand. "I'm on my third latte."

That ought to help her with her relaxation poses, Renita thought.

"Renita," Brett said from behind her.

She set the coffee down on a table, unprepared for

how much it would hurt to see him. "I know you're busy, but do you have a few minutes?"

"Come through to my office." He led the way up the stairs to his new office and shut the door, muffling the noise.

Renita glanced around. He'd framed his Collingwood jersey and hung it on the wall alongside a photo of his team. The furniture was new. "You've done a good job with the refurbishment."

"Thanks," Brett said quietly. The irony of how it came about couldn't have been lost on him. "What can I do for you?"

"Give me a dollar." She held out her hand, palm up.

"What is this for?" Brett said, fishing in his pocket. He placed a dollar coin in her hand.

Renita opened her purse and took out the leather case with his Brownlow Medal. "Now you've bought it back. You'll pay me the full amount when you can. In the meantime, I'll feel better if it's in your possession."

She could see him struggling with himself. It went against a lifetime of O'Connor pride to accept what must seem like charity.

"I can't take it," he said, pushing it back at her. "You own the medal, that dollar notwithstanding."

"Don't you get it, Brett? It was never about the money." She placed the case on his desk. "I'm giving you your Brownlow Medal because I love you."

His gaze faltered. "Renita—"

She pressed on, speaking faster to get it all out before she lost courage. "I want what's best for you even if it means—" Her voice broke. "I—I lose you." She held up a hand. "I know. I already have."

Her eyes were welling. She had to wrap this up quickly. She took a piece of paper out of her purse, the receipt she'd prepared. "This proves the Brownlow Medal is your property."

Brett took it reluctantly, clearly troubled. "I'll pay you back as soon as I settle with Amber. If that doesn't work out, I'll make payments just as if it was a loan."

"If the scene downstairs is anything to go by, you're on to a winner here. You know, Brett, I have to admit, you were right. The exercise machines are a hit. You'll figure out the business end or you'll hire someone who can do your accounts. You'll be a success because you have the right touch with people."

"Renita, I—I don't know what to say."

Smiling through her tears, she backed up, found the door handle and fumbled it open.

Then she was on the other side, shutting the door, leaving him behind. As she quickly made her way to the exit she heard Tegan calling her.

Renita kept walking.

BRETT LAY ON THE BENCH and gripped the loaded barbell. Sweat dripped off his temples and snaked down his neck. Tightening his core muscles, he focused and pushed, grunting as he pressed two hundred pounds.

The grand opening had been a roaring success. Over a hundred new members had signed up in the two weeks since. He'd had to hire another full-time instructor and he'd added three new specialty classes with out-of-house instructors.

He ought to be happy.

Renita's face as she'd given him back his medal—brave, hurt—flashed into his mind. He faltered. The bar crashed back into the cradle.

He squeezed his eyes shut, not knowing if it was anger or regret that was causing this pain in his chest.

How could she not understand that giving him two hundred thousand dollars would destroy their relationship? Then, to add insult to injury, she'd given him back his medal for a dollar.

"Brett, sorry to disturb you, but you still haven't looked over the revised group fitness program before I print it up." Janet rustled a piece of paper next to his head.

He didn't respond. This was a minor detail; she didn't need his approval.

Janet touched his shoulder. "Brett! You in there?"

"I heard. Just put the program on the seat of the leg press." He waited a moment until she'd had time to go, then ducked his head under the barbell and came to a seated position, his legs straddling the bench.

She was still there, arms crossed, waiting.

With a sigh, he glanced over the program, then handed it back to her. "It looks fine." Janet didn't budge. "By the way, thanks for picking up the slack these past few days. I've had some personal issues."

"I don't mind taking on your clients, or even running the whole gym," Janet said. "But overexercising isn't the answer to whatever's eating you. It's bad for your body *and* your mind. You know it."

Exercise had always been his salvation, his happy place when the going got rough. When he'd caught Amber cheating he'd practically lived at the gym, working out for hours every day. Until his aching joints and fatigued body forced him to take a break. And now, with Renita, it was the same story all over again.

Brett wiped his face and neck with a towel. "I know what I'm doing."

"Are you going to tell me what's wrong?" When he didn't answer Janet eased onto the seat of the leg press. "It's Renita, isn't it? You've had a fight or something. That's why I'm training her now."

"I don't want to talk about it." He pushed a hand through his damp hair.

"Okay, fine." Janet rose. "Just a heads-up…she's coming in this afternoon for a session."

"I'll get changed and go." Wincing, he got to his feet slowly, babying his bad knee. It hadn't bothered him for months. Now, through overwork, it was acting up again. Janet was right. He had to stop.

RUNNING LATE, Renita hurried up the stairs at Puccini's Bistro to the private function room where the Chamber of Commerce breakfast was being held. She could hear the buzz of conversation and the clink of ceramic cups on saucers. The smells of coffee and warm pastries drifted down to her, stirring the ever-present hunger in her stomach.

She came through the doorway, her smile in place. Just because her life had fallen into a hole and she felt like crap didn't mean she could opt out of the networking group she'd help grow into a real force in the community.

She paused, scanning the group of twenty-odd men and women standing around with coffee, chatting before breakfast. She froze.

By the windows across the room, talking to Norm, the owner of the athletic store, stood Brett. In a dark blazer over jeans and an open neck shirt, he looked masculine and healthy and utterly gorgeous.

Her heart contracted painfully in her chest. This must be some kind of nightmare.

Brett saw her and stumbled in his conversation, his coffee cup clattering into the saucer he held in his other hand.

Like an automaton, Renita smiled and nodded,

then turned to talk to whoever was closest. To her relief, it happened to be her brother, Jack. "What are *you* doing here?"

"You invited me to attend weeks ago," Jack said. "You urged me to join the Chamber of Commerce and to attend today's talk. You said it would be vitally useful in growing my business."

She'd said the same things to Brett. "Remind me in the future not to be such a civic cheerleader."

"What's wrong?" Jack said. "You look terrible."

"Thanks, darling brother. I feel sick." She met his gaze. "Brett and I broke up."

"Oh, hell. I'm sorry to hear that." Jack gave her a quick hug. "Are you okay?"

"No." Before she could say anything else, Darcy Newton, the owner of the Summerside pub, came up to them.

"Hey, Renita," Darcy said, grinning broadly. "I heard you gave a standout karaoke performance at Poppy's birthday party." He nudged Jack in the ribs. "Your sister missed her calling. She should have been a rock diva."

"Ha, ha," Renita said, faking a good-natured laugh. She was relieved when Jack, instead of ribbing her as he normally would have, directed the conversation to a new brand of draft beer Darcy was offering.

Renita pretended to listen to Jack and Darcy while watching Brett surreptitiously, aware of his every move. He took a piece of melon from the fruit plate on the table. She noted the strong flexing of his jaw as he chewed. Only a few days ago she'd kissed that mouth.

Their situation was messy. Brett was a member of the business community of Summerside now. She would see him regularly at functions like this, and around the village. And he was her brother's friend and her father's personal trainer. Lexie thought he was the best. Sienna acted as if she could hear wedding bells—and not just her own. Hetty…well, she wasn't in the picture these days.

Out of the corner of her eye Renita saw Brett clap a hand on Norm's shoulder. Then he started toward her.

She turned to Jack, but he was talking with someone else. At that precise moment everyone in the room was busy conversing. Then Brett was right there, so close she could smell his aftershave and see the whorls in his faint reddish stubble.

He stood beside her, looking out at the room. "This is awkward."

All of a sudden she felt a surge of anger. This was *her* town, her family. "I'm not leaving."

"Nor am I. I'm here for the talk," he said adamantly.

A spoon clanging on a coffee cup got everyone's attention. Theresa, Summerside's forty-something mayor, said above the hubbub, "Everyone, please take a seat where your name tag is. While we eat we'll listen to Mr. George Marshall speak about business planning for growth."

Renita made her way to the long table covered in white linen, scanning the name tags for her place. Finding it, she pulled out a chair— Oh, great. Brett was right beside her. Half a dozen words she couldn't say aloud in front of the Chamber of Commerce ran through her head.

"What's with the place tags?" Brett said, taking his seat.

"Someone's bright idea to facilitate networking," Renita muttered as they sat down. Hers, in fact, but that had been a year ago, long before Brett ever came back to Summerside.

Chamber of Commerce breakfasts usually flew by in a stream of conversation and exchange of news. This morning the minutes dragged. Renita couldn't focus on the talk, given by a nationally prominent businessman. While Brett took notes, she pushed her food around her plate and pretended to eat. The mushroom omelet tasted like sawdust. She was hyperaware of Brett, every movement, every sound, the shift of his thigh, the flexing of his fingers as his pen moved across the page of his notebook.

They reached for the water jug at the same time. She felt the electricity of his touch right down to her bones.

He jerked back, angling his chair away. "Sorry."

"It's okay." She gritted her teeth.

"Renita, you've hardly touched your food," Theresa

said from across the table. "Is something wrong with it?"

"It's delicious." She took a bite, but her throat felt blocked. She couldn't swallow. "Excuse me," she mumbled. Pushing back her chair, she half ran, half stumbled from the room.

The ladies' room was empty, thank God. She collapsed on the closed lid of the toilet and dropped her head in her hands. Her heart was hammering in her chest as she fought back tears. Damn. She couldn't just leave. She'd forgotten her purse on the back of her chair in the restaurant.

Someone knocked on her cubicle door. It was probably Theresa. "I'm fine. I'll be out in a minute."

"It's me." Brett added in a low voice, "I'm taking off. I pretended to get a text from Tegan."

"You can't come in here. This is the women's restroom," Renita hissed. Looking down, she could see the toes of his black leather shoes.

"Here's your purse." He slid it under the door.

Renita clamped her jaw shut.

"Renita. Are you all right?"

She stood and opened the door. "I'm fine."

"I told Theresa you were coming down with something," he went on. "Gives you an out if you want to take it."

"I—I'll go back in. As long as you're leaving."

"I heard what I came for. The networking can wait." Brett raised his hand as if to touch her cheek. Then his fingers curled and he dropped his hand.

Renita brushed past him, getting an agonizing whiff of his aftershave, and pushed through the door to the landing. She took a moment to compose herself before going back in to the meeting. She heard uneven footsteps descending the stairs, and cocked her head to listen. Was he limping? Before she could make up her mind, the door of the restaurant opened, and then closed with a quiet snick.

CHAPTER FIFTEEN

"COME TO MAMMA, big boy." Tears blurred Renita's vision as she stuck her arm inside the aviary and braced herself for Frankie's weight. Lucy sat at her feet, her soft fur brushing Renita's bare leg. Johnny prowled the shady recesses beneath the bushes.

The cockatoo crab-walked onto Renita's forearm. His bright yellow crest lifted as he eyed her. "Crybaby! Crybaby!"

She choked out a laugh even as she began to cry. Sensing her distress, Lucy licked her knee.

Dogs didn't break your heart; birds might insult you, but they didn't know what they were saying. Cats…well, cats simply assumed you were as independent as they were.

Okay, she'd made a mistake. Couldn't Brett see she'd done it from the best of motivations—love? Everyone had insecurities, him included. If he loved her, he should be able to let his guard down, accept her help.

Oh, she understood his view—that if she loved him, she should have respected his wishes and protected his pride. Yet she'd shown him her vulnerable side, and he couldn't do the same. Which left them at an impasse.

She glanced at her watch and carried Frankie back to the aviary. It was time to get ready to go to the clinic. Her breast surgery was scheduled for that day. Even though Brett hadn't been supportive, she'd hoped he'd be there for her when she needed some TLC. That wasn't going to happen now.

She left for the mall early so she didn't have time to mope at home. Besides, fasting for the anesthetic, she was starving. She needed to get away from the fridge.

Every woman she knew swore by retail therapy. Maybe that would do the trick for her, too. But an hour later she was listlessly picking through the racks, completely uninterested in the fashions that now fit her. Maybe she would even cancel the surgery. What was the point of looking good if she wasn't with Brett?

Dumb attitude. Being single was all the more reason to make an effort. She forced herself to buy a new top and skirt and some strappy sandals. While she was at it she bought a purse. As soon as she'd signed the credit card slip, she was hit with guilt and remorse. Shopping hadn't made her feel better. And a new dress was an extravagance she could no longer afford.

Buying Brett's Brownlow Medal had increased her mortgage payments substantially. Now she would struggle to pay for extras like this breast surgery. And she didn't have any backup savings in case she lost her job. For someone who wasn't a risk-taker this kind of vulnerability was truly scary.

At the appointed time she made her way to the clinic and was admitted. A nurse named Marisa in a pale blue fitted uniform showed her to a room with a hospital bed and gave her a green gown that opened at the front. The smell of antiseptic tickled her throat and the stark white fluorescent bulbs made her squint.

She got changed and lay on the bed. Dr. Renfrew, the surgeon she'd met at her initial consultation, breezed in, accompanied by Marisa. In his green scrubs, he was a boyish-looking man in his forties with a chatty bedside manner.

"How are you doing, Renita? Good?" Barely waiting for her nod, he delicately opened her gown, holding her gaze as he talked. "We'll get you prepped. We're just waiting for the anesthetist. It won't be long before Marisa will bring you into O.R."

Marisa handed him the surgical marker and with a practiced hand Dr. Renfrew swiftly but carefully inked dotted lines around her nipples where the incisions for the implants would be made. "All done." He smiled at her, squeezed her shoulder and breezed out.

Marisa handed her a magazine. "You can sit up, if you like. It won't be long," she repeated, then left the room.

Renita waited, leafing through the magazine. Every few minutes she checked her watch. Hopping up, she paced the linoleum in her paper slippers. What was taking so long? She wanted to get this over with before she changed her mind.

Before she changed her mind?

The thought stopped her cold. Was she afraid of going under the knife?

Well, who in their right mind wouldn't be?

Renita went to the mirror and pulled aside her gown to look at the purple markings on her breasts.

Cut on dotted line.

She'd seen plastic surgery performed on TV. The surgeon's knife slicing through skin and into flesh. She shivered. Beads of blood formed along the incision, the doctor pulled back the skin and muscle layer.... Ugh.

She flexed her pectoral muscles like a bodybuilder, then turned sideways to study her profile.

Okay, so her breasts couldn't compare to Pammy's. Or Amber's, for that matter. Sure, if they were bigger they'd be more in proportion to her hips. But they weren't *that* small.

"What is this obsession with being perfect?" Was she obsessed? Or did she just want to look her best? Nothing wrong with that.

But why the sudden focus on her breasts?

Brett hadn't cared about their size. Why did she?

Her extra weight had always been a source of

insecurity. Now that she'd trimmed down she should be gaining confidence. No sooner had she lost weight than she'd started worrying over the size of her breasts. After she got them "fixed" what would be next?

She'd done the psychological assessment required prior to cosmetic surgery, blithely writing down what she figured the counselor wanted to hear. Maybe she should have thought this through more thoroughly before she'd signed on the dotted line.

Dotted lines.

All of a sudden she wanted to scrub her skin, get rid of the purple markings—evidence that she didn't like herself.

Losing weight and getting fit were good things.

Surgery to enlarge her breasts so a man would think she was attractive…dumb.

Worse, she was being a coward where Brett was concerned. And she didn't like cowards. All of a sudden she was angry. Angry at herself, angry at him. They'd had a chance for something special and they'd both screwed it up, her for fear of getting hurt, him for his stupid macho pride.

Marisa, ageless with her smooth forehead and slender figure, came into the room pushing a gurney. "The anesthetist is here. If you'll hop on the gurney, I'll take you into the operating room."

"I've changed my mind," Renita said. "I don't want breast surgery. I want to go home."

THE SHRIEKS AND LAUGHTER of Brett's young nephews and nieces playing footy filled his parents' backyard. Ryan and Tom stood on the sidelines, bottles of beer in their hands. Over by the garage Hal was barbecuing lamb chops and sausages.

"Go play with the other kids," Brett said to Tegan. "I need to talk to your grandpa."

"I'm not a kid and I never liked playing football," Tegan said. She went off and he watched as she volunteered to help the women bring out the food and drinks.

Brett grabbed a cold bottle of beer and set a package of thick rib-eye steaks still wrapped in butcher's paper on the apron of the barbecue. "Hey, Dad. How's it going?"

"We heard your grand opening was a success. Well done." Hal switched the barbecue tongs to his other hand and clapped Brett on the back. He tore open the steaks and started placing them on the grill. "What are you doing driving a Ford? Is the Mercedes in the shop?"

"I traded it in." Brett took an envelope from his pocket and handed it over. "Here's your five thousand."

Hal's smile faded. He made no move to take the money. "You weren't supposed to know about that."

"You weren't supposed to be hit up for cash."

Brett tucked the envelope in the pocket of his dad's barbecue apron. "I don't need help."

"Course you don't." But his dad seemed troubled. "Your mother was hoping you'd bring Renita with you today. Didn't she mention it?"

"Renita and I aren't together." The words were like a switch that activated a pain in Brett's chest. "Excuse me, Dad. I have to talk to Tom."

He strode across the grass to his brothers. "Hey, guys." Brett handed a folded piece of paper to Tom. "Could you have a look and tell me if the numbers on this loan repayment plan make sense?"

"You did this?" Tom asked, glancing over the spreadsheet.

"That's why I'd like it checked. And don't bother suggesting I pay it back over a longer period than five years. That's not a mistake. I want this debt off my hands as quickly as possible."

"Let me sit down," Tom said. "I'll go get a calculator." Pulling his reading glasses out of his shirt pocket, he headed into the house.

Ryan glanced over his sunglasses at Brett. "I presume this is about that bit of financial strife you got into with the equipment. Was it worth it in the end?"

Brett nodded. "For the viability of the gym, yes. A thousand times, yes."

For his personal life? Not so much.

He didn't want to think about that. Handing his beer to Ryan, he ran out into the game. "Hey, kids, let me show you how to pass that ball."

"Yay, Uncle Brett!" A chorus of cheers greeted him as he was mobbed by his nephews.

He spent the next thirty minutes giving them tips. Then he retired to the sidelines to reclaim his beer, by now gone warm. He was getting a second beer from the cooler when Tom returned and handed him back his spreadsheet.

"Nothing wrong with your calculations. But between mortgage and loan payments you'll be eating beans and rice every day for the next five years."

"I'll survive." Brett folded the paper and tucked it back in his pocket. "Thanks, mate."

Later that night he unlocked the door to the house and let Tegan precede him inside. He was worn-out from a long week, and his footsteps echoed on the marble tiles in the huge foyer. It was a lonely sound.

Brett tried to brush that aside, turning his thoughts back to the rollicking time they'd had at his parents' place. But the vivid images of three generations crammed into the tiny home only made his palatial house seem more…empty.

Tegan went upstairs to get ready for bed. Brett roamed, ending up at the window overlooking the bay. For once the view of the city lights didn't console him. The emptiness wasn't just inside the house. It was in him.

Restlessly, he moved through the quiet rooms to the kitchen. Sliding glass doors opened onto a small backyard crammed with shrubs and wrought-iron benches that were too uncomfortable to sit on. No room here for kids to play football.

He loved Renita. He wanted her back.

Five years was too long to wait.

He needed to learn to be patient. But not that patient.

He pulled his Brownlow Medal out of his pocket and opened the leather case to study the intricate scrollwork in the glow of the security light. He could call up Simon Toltz and sell it again.

But that felt wrong. It wasn't just that he wanted to keep his medal—which he did, very badly—but selling it would negate the sacrifice Renita had made for him.

"Dad?" Tegan stood in the doorway in her pajamas, ghostly pale in the moonlight streaming through the kitchen window. "Are you okay?"

Funny how things could come to you in a flash. He'd been kidding himself that he clung to this big house for Tegan's sake…. He'd done it for himself, to show the world what he'd achieved. Ever since he was a teenager he'd struggled to escape his parents' poverty, make something of himself. He'd had the big house, the fancy car, the six-figure income. None of it had made him happy.

"I'm going to sell the house," he said to Tegan. "With a smaller mortgage I'll be able to pay Renita back sooner. What do you think?"

"That's good." She fiddled with the hem of her pajama top. "Then will you and she start seeing each other again?"

"I don't know." The lightness of a moment ago deserted him as quickly as it had come. "I'm not sure she'll want me after some of the things I've said."

"Do you love her?"

Slowly, Brett nodded. "Yes, I do. It's taken me a while to realize just how much."

Tegan tiptoed in bare feet over the cold tiles and put her arms around his waist. "Then you should tell her."

THE DOORBELL RANG while Brett was putting on his running shorts and sleeveless tee for the Fun Run.

"Tegan!" Brett called down. "Can you get that?"

Three weeks had passed since the grand opening. The gym continued to thrive. He'd started an online accounting course. His house had just sold. Changes were in motion.

He hadn't said anything to Renita yet. But finally his life was in order and everything was in place.

"Okay, Dad." A moment later she gave a surprised squeal. "Mum! What are you doing here?"

"I thought I'd drop in and see how you're doing," Amber said.

Brett grabbed his windbreaker and went downstairs.

Amber wore a miniskirt and a halter top that ended north of her belly button. Her long hair was a shiny platinum and her nails were green. The tattoo of a winged dragon wound sinuously up her left arm.

"What's going on in the village?" she said. "It looks like the circus has come to town."

"Today's the Fun Run. Do you want to enter? Maybe if you do, Tegan will reconsider."

"No, thanks." She shuddered. "Tegan, honey, you can show me the best place in town for ice cream."

"There *is* only one place. But it's good. We can watch the end of the Fun Run from there," Tegan said. "I'll get changed." She ran off, ponytail swinging.

"I can't believe you've made the hour-long journey out here to the 'sticks,'" Brett said.

Twirling her oversize white sunglasses, Amber strolled into the living room. "I came to get a look at this house you're selling."

"Sold," Brett corrected. "Properties with a view, close to the beach, go fast. Just yesterday I signed the transfer papers."

She picked up a Maori wood carving and smoothed a thumb over the polished surface. "Have you found another place?"

"I bought a house not far from where my parents live. It's a bit run-down, but it's got a big backyard."

"Run-down?" Amber made a face. "Tegan's not used to roughing it."

"I've got debts to pay. I'll enjoy fixing it up a little at a time."

Amber put down the carving. "I heard you had to sell your Brownlow Medal. That must have hurt."

"Old news." He jammed his hands in his pockets. "Do you want a cold drink or something?"

"I didn't come all this way just for ice cream, Brett. I'm ready to settle. Screw the lawyers. If we keep going like this there'll be nothing left for either of us."

Brett closed his eyes. "You couldn't have come to this conclusion six months ago?"

"When I read in the newspaper about your Brownlow Medal I realized what I was doing to you."

"You never cared what you were costing me before."

"Tegan had a go at me the last time she stayed for the weekend." Amber's expression was full of regret. "I've made mistakes. I haven't been a very good example to her. She worships *you*."

"Well, I'm glad you've decided to be reasonable, Amber. Better late than never."

"So you don't need to sell your house."

Brett thought about going back to his flashy lifestyle. Just for a moment he was tempted. But with the end of his football career, the end of his marriage to Amber, he wasn't that guy anymore. "I'm still going to."

"Whatever," Amber said with a shrug. "I'll have Tegan back in a few hours. Is that okay?"

"She can show you the house on your way. Don't be put off by the exterior. It's much nicer inside."

In fact, it was worse, but he didn't want Amber to think he wasn't taking proper care of their daughter.

FLAGS WERE FLYING down Main Street and the high school band played in the village square. Crowds lined the sidewalks and spilled into the blocked-off roads.

Renita jogged on the spot next to her dad, who was stretching out his quads. Like the other runners, they wore official bibs with their registration numbers over their T-shirt.

She glanced up at the clouds, now darkening over the bay. "The forecast only called for showers."

"The weatherman revised that to a possible thunderstorm," Steve replied. "The front moving in looks ugly."

Renita tried to find familiar faces and recognized members from the gym and some clients from the bank, as well as a few of her coworkers. No Brett. She wasn't sure if she was relieved or disappointed.

She'd had little contact with him in the past month, other than seeing him in passing at the gym. He'd paid back his parents and Jack, and he'd promised to repay her in full as soon as he could. She hardly cared about the money. She wanted her pal back.

"Have you seen our fearless leader this morning?" she said to her father.

"He'll be here," Steve said. "He wouldn't miss the run."

Lexie, her long blond hair a mass of curls in the humidity, pushed through the crowd. "Hetty's here. She's come to see you run, Dad. Over there in front of the greengrocer."

Renita picked out her mother by her short gray hair. When Hetty saw them looking her way, she smiled and waved.

"Huh. Now she shows up," Steve muttered.

"Go say hello," Renita urged, giving him a nudge.

"Why should I?"

"Maybe she wants to reconcile. *Go,* Dad."

"Hey, you two." Brett wove his way over and clapped a hand on Steve's shoulder. "Looking fit, mate! Remember what I said about pacing yourself."

"I remember." Steve turned his back on Hetty. "I don't forget easily."

Renita tore her gaze away from her mum's disappointed expression to find Brett still standing there. With a struggle she forced a smile. *Don't let him know he hurt you.*

"Good luck." He squeezed her shoulder and leaned down to kiss her lightly on the lips.

What was he doing, kissing her? She searched his face, but another runner claimed his attention.

Her emotions were churning as the organizer called over the loudspeaker, "Participants, find your places. When the gun goes, you're off!"

Confusion reigned as the runners jostled for position. Brett went up to the front of the pack with Jack. Sienna was somewhere in the middle. Renita and Steve trailed with the less fit crowd.

The starting gun fired. With the blast still ringing in her ears, Renita began to run. Glancing sideways at her father, she grinned. "Did you ever think we'd be doing this?"

Steve grinned back, alert behind his steel-framed glasses. "Not in a million years. I'm stoked."

"Stoked?" Renita laughed. Her dad had taken ten years off his attitude in the past three months.

She stopped talking then, saving her breath for the run. The route would take them in a large, roughly rectangular circuit from the village center up to the highway, north for a few miles, then west to the water before running south along the Cliff Road. Finally, they would head up a long, steep hill back to the village square.

She could have gone faster, but she chugged along with Steve. They both needed the moral support. Half an hour in, the heavens opened and the rain that had been threatening all morning poured down. Renita's legs were burning and mud-splattered as she splashed through a puddle. With her hair plastered in her eyes she couldn't see beyond the bobbing backs immediately in front of her. Steve huffed and puffed alongside her. His glasses were fogged and patches of red stood out on his cheeks.

Renita got a stitch in her side as they turned south along Cliff Road in the opposite direction to Brett's house near the end of the cul de sac. The wind whistled over the gray, choppy water, buffeting her. Lightning streaked against the black clouds fifty miles away, on the far side of the bay, followed by the distant rumble of thunder.

The stitch in her side got worse. She pressed on. Ahead of her loomed the big hill leading back to the highway. For the first time Renita wasn't sure she could complete this. Shielding her eyes, she peered through the pelting rain. The runners had spread out, the leaders already halfway up the hill.

Members of the Rotary Club were handing out cups of water at the side of the road. Renita motioned to Steve and they pulled out of the crowd to have a drink. Her hand shook as she gulped the cool liquid. Tossing the empty cup in the bin, she bent over, palms hot on her rain-wet knees, lungs heaving. She thought about how easy it would be to duck down a side street and walk home.

A hand touched her shoulder. "How are you feeling?" It was Brett.

She lifted her head. "Like I want to die."

"You're doing great. You, too, Steve. Way to go, both of you."

Steve nodded, too winded to speak.

"Why aren't you up at the front, leading the pack?" Renita asked.

"I'll run with you and Steve for a while."

"Mr. Impatience bringing up the rear? That'll be a first."

"Never mind the back talk. Are you ready to go again?"

She straightened, shook out her legs. "I'm ready."

They started jogging up the steep hill. Renita pushed herself so she wouldn't hold Brett back too much. Steve fell behind a few paces to join another older man who was also struggling. Steve waved at her to go on without him. The rain continued to pelt down. The exertion required all Renita's breath, but her curiosity was worse than the burning in her lungs.

"What was that kiss about?" she gasped. "Have you decided not to be all macho football player and admit that you needed help?"

"I'm an *ex*-football player," Brett reminded her.

"You can't go around giving me run-by smooches. I've gone through fifty kinds of hell because of you." Out of breath, her thighs screaming with pain, she had to slow to a walk. "I was *over* you."

Brett slowed, too. "Are you still? Over me, that is?"

In the driving rain, with her hair plastered to her face, her clothes sticking to her body, she stared at him. He wasn't being facetious. He wanted to know.

The hell with him. She couldn't say it again.

She started to run once more.

"I love you!" Brett shouted from behind her, above the driving rain. "I want us to try again."

Renita stopped. She should have more pride than to throw herself into his arms. But she didn't. Her arms went around his neck, and he picked her up and whirled her around before setting her back down and taking her mouth in a kiss so hot that she was sure steam must be rising from their lips.

Renita was dimly aware of runners streaming by them. She caught a glimpse of Steve, head bent, glasses fogged, race-walking past with his new buddy. The rain poured down relentlessly, soaking her through to the skin. She was sore all over, but in the freezing cold she was warm and happy.

At last she eased back, breaking the kiss. "If we don't get moving we're going to be last over the finish line."

Brett brushed her wet hair off her forehead, kissed her dripping cheeks and her nose. "I don't care."

"Well, I do. I've worked for this."

She began to run again, her feet pounding the pavement, one in front of the other, up the long hill. As she neared the crest, she increased her pace, spurred on by a burst of energy. At last she staggered over the top onto level ground.

"The worst is over." Brett wasn't even breathing hard. "Just three miles to go."

The worst was over. He was right about that.

"You go on ahead," she said, knowing his competitive nature. "I'll see you at the village square."

"I'm not leaving. Get used to it." He glanced down at her chest, where her wet T-shirt and bib were glued like a second skin. "You didn't get the implants."

"I...changed my mind at the last minute." In spite of herself, she looked for his reaction.

He gave it to her in one emphatic word. "Good!"

Grinning, Renita plowed doggedly on. She and Brett didn't talk after that, but it helped having him beside her. They caught up with Steve and jogged beside him and his new friend for a while before gradually pulling ahead. The rain eased, the sun came out and her shoes stopped squelching. From somewhere she got a second wind as she turned away from the highway and down Summerside Road on the last leg of the run, heading into the village.

As they crossed the finish line, Brett got separated from her by other runners, town dignitaries and Fun Run sponsors.

"Party at the gym," he called to her over the sea of heads. "To celebrate completing the run."

Someone was calling Brett's name. A woman.

Renita glanced over and recognized Amber from magazine photos. What did *she* want?

Renita turned to her father, surrounded by his mates from the Men's Shed. She fought her way through the scrum to give him a high five.

Steve whooped and scooped her up in his arm. "We did it, chicken! We ran ten miles!"

Renita hugged him tightly. "It feels damn good."

RENITA STOOD wrapped in a towel in front of her closet. The sexy red dress or the slinky black? She was reaching for the red when she caught herself. The party was at a gym, not a nightclub. Just because she looked better than she ever had in her life didn't mean she had to show off her figure every time she stepped outside.

But Amber was in town. Renita had to compete—

No, she didn't. Brett had divorced Amber for very good reasons. Renita didn't want to look like her. She wanted to look like herself, her *best* self.

The party at the gym was like the grand opening all over again. Renita had to park down the street because the gym lot was overflowing with cars. Loud music was playing and dozens of people milled about the refreshment area, drinking champagne and munching on catered finger food.

Brett must have sensed her presence, because the moment she walked in he turned to her.

Wearing her glasses and a blue T-shirt and jeans,

she watched for his reaction. He set down his glass and came toward her.

"I did it," she said. "I ran ten miles."

"I knew you could." He took her hand. "Come to my office. I have something for you."

As Renita followed him up the stairs, she couldn't help but recall the last time they'd done this, and the horrible way that had ended. But things were different now. She didn't quite understand what had changed, but was just glad to be back with Brett.

He let her into the office and closed the door, then went to his desk and took out a slip of paper. It was a bank check made out in her name, for a hundred ninety thousand dollars. "I sold my house."

"You what!" She dropped into a chair, stunned. "I didn't even know it was for sale. Are you leaving Summerside?" He couldn't. He'd just told her he loved her.

"Are you kidding? After everything I went through for the gym? I'm committed to this town."

Flooded with relief, she shook her head. "Don't just spring things on me like that. What about Tegan and her sailing lessons?"

"Turns out she doesn't like sailing. Go figure." Brett shrugged. "So, do you reckon we're square?"

"I don't know." Recovering, she glanced at the check again. "There's a mistake." She met his startled gaze with a smile. "It should be one hundred eighty-nine thousand, nine hundred and ninety-nine dollars…. You already paid me a dollar."

He let out a bark of laughter. Then bent his head to kiss her, and bumped her glasses. "Why are you wearing these things? They get in the way."

"Not so fast." She pushed the glasses farther up her nose. "What did Amber want?"

"We settled the terms of divorce." He pulled her into his arms. "I love *you,* Renita. I love you for who you are inside, thin or fat, hot or not. Will you have me?"

Her heart filled her chest so completely she could barely breathe. The backs of her eyes burned, but this was no moment for tears.

"I bought another house," Brett said. "Yours is nicer, but this one is bigger. The best thing I can say about it is it's got a huge backyard."

She eased back, blinking. He was talking about moving in together. It hit her then that if she said yes, she'd be giving up her old life for good—the house she'd scrimped and saved for, her independence…

"Is there room for an aviary?" she asked.

"We can have a goddamn zoo if you want." He was very still, waiting for her answer, waiting as if his life depended on it.

"Okay, then." She couldn't speak for the lump in her throat.

His dazzling blue eyes seemed to swallow her whole. "This is it, isn't it, Renita? Our love is real. *You're* real."

"Yes," she said, nodding and blinking. "I'm real."

It was the nicest compliment he could have paid her.

* * * * *

Don't miss the final book
in Joan Kilby's SUMMERSIDE STORIES.
Be sure to check out Lexie's story,
TWO AGAINST THE ODDS,
wherever Harlequin books are sold!

Harlequin
Super Romance

COMING NEXT MONTH

Available March 8, 2011

#1692 BONE DEEP
Count on a Cop
Janice Kay Johnson

#1693 TWO AGAINST THE ODDS
Summerside Stories
Joan Kilby

#1694 THE PAST BETWEEN US
Mama Jo's Boys
Kimberly Van Meter

#1695 NOTHING BUT THE TRUTH
Project Justice
Kara Lennox

#1696 FOR BABY AND ME
9 Months Later
Margaret Watson

#1697 WITH A LITTLE HELP
Make Me a Match
Valerie Parv

REQUEST YOUR FREE BOOKS!

2 FREE NOVELS
PLUS
2 FREE GIFTS!

ROMANTIC
SUSPENSE

Sparked by Danger, Fueled by Passion.

YES! Please send me 2 FREE Silhouette® Romantic Suspense novels and my 2 FREE gifts (gifts are worth about $10). After receiving them, if I don't wish to receive any more books, I can return the shipping statement marked "cancel." If I don't cancel, I will receive 4 brand-new novels every month and be billed just $4.24 per book in the U.S. or $4.99 per book in Canada. That's a saving of at least 15% off the cover price! It's quite a bargain! Shipping and handling is just 50¢ per book in the U.S. and 75¢ per book in Canada.* I understand that accepting the 2 free books and gifts places me under no obligation to buy anything. I can always return a shipment and cancel at any time. Even if I never buy another book, the two free books and gifts are mine to keep forever.

240/340 SDN FC95

Name	(PLEASE PRINT)

Address	Apt. #

City	State/Prov.	Zip/Postal Code

Signature (if under 18, a parent or guardian must sign)

Mail to the **Reader Service**:
IN U.S.A.: P.O. Box 1867, Buffalo, NY 14240-1867
IN CANADA: P.O. Box 609, Fort Erie, Ontario L2A 5X3

Not valid for current subscribers to Silhouette Romantic Suspense books.

Want to try two free books from another line?
Call 1-800-873-8635 or visit www.ReaderService.com.

* Terms and prices subject to change without notice. Prices do not include applicable taxes. Sales tax applicable in N.Y. Canadian residents will be charged applicable taxes. Offer not valid in Quebec. This offer is limited to one order per household. All orders subject to credit approval. Credit or debit balances in a customer's account(s) may be offset by any other outstanding balance owed by or to the customer. Please allow 4 to 6 weeks for delivery. Offer available while quantities last.

Your Privacy—The Reader Service is committed to protecting your privacy. Our Privacy Policy is available online at www.ReaderService.com or upon request from the Reader Service.

We make a portion of our mailing list available to reputable third parties that offer products we believe may interest you. If you prefer that we not exchange your name with third parties, or if you wish to clarify or modify your communication preferences, please visit us at www.ReaderService.com/consumerschoice or write to us at Reader Service Preference Service, P.O. Box 9062, Buffalo, NY 14269. Include your complete name and address.

SRSII

USA TODAY *bestselling author Lynne Graham*
is back with a thrilling new trilogy
SECRETLY PREGNANT, CONVENIENTLY WED

*Three heroines must marry alpha males to keep
their dreams…but Alejandro, Angelo and Cesario
are not about to be tamed!*

Book 1—JEMIMA'S SECRET
Available March 2011 from Harlequin Presents®.

JEMIMA yanked open a drawer in the sideboard to find
Alfie's birth certificate. Her son was her husband's child.
It was a question of telling the truth whether she liked it or
not. She extended the certificate to Alejandro.

"This has to be nonsense," Alejandro asserted.

"Well, if you can find some other way of explaining how
I managed to give birth by that date and Alfie not be yours,
I'd like to hear it," Jemima challenged.

Alejandro glanced up, golden eyes bright as blades and
as dangerous. "All this proves is that you must still have
been pregnant when you walked out on our marriage. It
does not automatically follow that the child is mine."

"'I know it doesn't suit you to hear this news now and I
really didn't want to tell you. But I can't lie to you about it.
Someday Alfie may want to look you up and get acquainted."

"If what you have just told me is the truth, if that little
boy does prove to be mine, it was vindictive and extremely
selfish of you to leave me in ignorance!"

Jemima paled. "When I left you, I had no idea that I was
still pregnant."

"Two years is a long period of time, yet you made no
attempt to inform me that I might be a father. I will want
DNA tests to confirm your claim before I make any deci-

sion about what I want to do."

"Do as you like," she told him curtly. "*I* know who Alfie's father is and there has never been any doubt of his identity."

"I will make arrangements for the tests to be carried out and I will see you again when the result is available," Alejandro drawled with lashings of dark Spanish masculine reserve.

"I'll contact a solicitor and start the divorce," Jemima proffered in turn.

Alejandro's eyes narrowed in a piercing scrutiny that made her uncomfortable. "It would be foolish to do anything before we have that DNA result."

"I disagree," Jemima flashed back. "I should have applied for a divorce the minute I left you!"

Alejandro quirked an ebony brow. "And why didn't you?"

Jemima dealt him a fulminating glance but said nothing, merely moving past him to open her front door in a blunt invitation for him to leave.

"I'll be in touch," he delivered on the doorstep.

What is Alejandro's next move? Perhaps rekindling their marriage is the only solution! But will Jemima agree?

Find out in Lynne Graham's
exciting new romance
JEMIMA'S SECRET

Available March 2011
from Harlequin Presents®.

Start your Best Body today with these top 3 nutrition tips!

1. **SHOP THE PERIMETER OF THE GROCERY STORE:** The good stuff—fruits, veggies, lean proteins and dairy—always line the outer edges of the store. When you veer into the center aisles, you enter the temptation zone, where the unhealthy foods live.

2. **WATCH PORTION SIZES:** Most portion sizes in restaurants are nearly twice the size of a true serving and at home, it's easy to "clean your plate." Use these easy serving guidelines:
   - Protein: the palm of your hand
   - Grains or Fruit: a cup of your hand
   - Veggies: the palm of two open hands

3. **USE THE RAINBOW RULE FOR PRODUCE:** Your produce drawers should be filled with every color of fruits and vegetables. The greater the variety, the more vitamins and other nutrients you add to your diet.

Find these and many more helpful tips in

YOUR BEST BODY NOW

by

TOSCA RENO

WITH STACY BAKER

Bestselling Author of
THE EAT-CLEAN DIET®

Available wherever books are sold!

PRESENTING…THE SEVENTH ANNUAL
MORE THAN WORDS™ ANTHOLOGY

Five bestselling authors
Five real-life heroines

This year's Harlequin
More Than Words award
recipients have changed lives,
one good deed at a time. To
celebrate these real-life heroines,
some of Harlequin's most
acclaimed authors have honored
the winners by writing stories
inspired by these dedicated
women. Within the pages
of *More Than Words Volume 7*,
you will find novellas written
by Carly Phillips, Donna Hill
and Jill Shalvis—and online at
www.HarlequinMoreThanWords.com
you can also access stories by
Pamela Morsi and Meryl Sawyer.

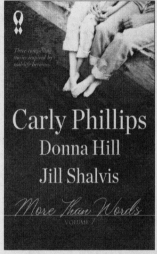

Coming soon in print and online!

Visit
www.HarlequinMoreThanWords.com
to access your FREE ebooks and to nominate
a real-life heroine in your community.

MTWV7763CS

HARLEQUIN®
Super Romance

Top author
Janice Kay Johnson

brings readers a riveting new romance
with

Bone Deep

Kathryn Riley is the prime suspect in
the case of her husband's disappearance
four years ago—that is, until someone tries
to make her disappear...forever. Now
handsome police chief Grant Haller must
stop suspecting Kathryn and instead begin
to protect her. But can Grant put aside the
growing feelings for Kathryn long enough
to catch the real criminal?

Find out in March.

Available wherever
books are sold.

HSR71692

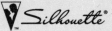

ROMANTIC

S U S P E N S E

Sparked by Danger, Fueled by Passion.

CARLA CASSIDY

Special Agent's Surrender

There's a killer on the loose in Black Rock,
and former FBI agent Jacob Grayson isn't about
to let Layla West become the next victim.

While she's hiding at the family ranch under Jacob's
protection, the desire between them burns hot.
But when the investigation turns personal,
their love and Layla's life are put on the line,
and the stakes have never been higher.

A brand-new tale of the

Available in March wherever books are sold!

Visit Silhouette Books at www.eHarlequin.com

SRS27718